THE AMERICAN CONQUEST
WINDOW TO THE HEART SAGA

JENNA BRANDT

This is a work of fiction. Names, characters, organizations, places, events and incidents are either products of the author's imagination or are used fictitiously. Locale and public names are sometimes used for atmospheric purposes. Any resemblance to actual persons, living or dead, actual events, or actual locations is purely coincidental. All rights reserved.

No part of this book may be reproduced, or stored in a retrieval system, or transmitted in any form or by any means, electronic, mechanical, photocopying, recording, or otherwise, without express written permission of the author, except in the case of brief quotations embodied in critical reviews and certain other noncommercial uses permitted by copyright law. For permission requests, email jenna@jennabrandt.com.

Text copyright © Jenna Brandt 2017.
Window to the Heart Saga © Jenna Brandt 2017.

CONTENTS

Prologue	1
Chapter 1	11
Chapter 2	24
Chapter 3	35
Chapter 4	54
Chapter 5	64
Chapter 6	78
Chapter 7	85
Chapter 8	103
Chapter 9	114
Chapter 10	125
Chapter 11	134
Chapter 12	141
Chapter 13	151
Chapter 14	158
Chapter 15	163
Chapter 16	171
Chapter 17	176
Chapter 18	180
Chapter 19	184
Chapter 20	192
Chapter 21	199
Chapter 22	205
Chapter 23	213
Chapter 24	224
Chapter 25	236
Chapter 26	246
Chapter 27	253
Chapter 28	260

Chapter 29	269
Epilogue	284
Sneak Peek of The Oregon Pursuit	288
Sneak Peek of Lawfully Loved	297
A Note from the Author	305
Also by Jenna Brandt	307
Acknowledgments	313
About the Author	315

PRAISE FOR JENNA BRANDT

Jenna Brandt knows what her readers like and delivers it.

— LENDA BURNS, LONGTIME READER

I am always excited when I see a new book by Jenna Brandt.

— LORI DYKES, AMAZON CUSTOMER

Jenna Brandt is, in my estimation, the most gifted author of Christian fiction in this generation!

— PAULA ROSE MICHELSON, FELLOW AUTHOR

Ms. Brandt writes from the heart and you can feel it in every page turned.

— SANDRA SEWELL WHITE, LONGTIME READER

For more information about Jenna Brandt visit her on any of her websites.

Signup for Jenna Brandt's Newsletter

Visit her on Social Media:

www.JennaBrandt.com
www.facebook.com/JennaBrandtAuthor
Jenna Brandt's Reader Group
hwww.twitter.com/JennaDBrandt
http://www.instagram.com/Jennnathewriter

*To my children: Katherine, Julianne, Dylan, and Nicole.
You are the center of my heart and joy of my life.
Being your mother is my proudest achievement.*

PROLOGUE

1865 Paris, France

Why did this always happen? Why did she always loose the people she loved?

"Margaret, I need you to hear this. You and your son are the best things that have ever happened to me. I never knew I could love anyone as much as I love the two of you."

Her husband, Lord Michel Robineau, the Marquis de Badour, had been in and out of consciousness for the past two days. In the past hour, he had rallied, Margaret suspected to say goodbye.

"What am I going to do without you, Michel? You are everything to me. I need you."

"You are strong, Margaret, so strong, and I know you *can* survive without me. You will for Henry's sake. I want you to make me a promise. I want you to leave Europe and never come back. Take this and use it to start over," he handed her an envelope. "Go to America like you had planned and do not let your past define you."

"I will, Michel. Whatever you want, I will do it."

His breathing was slowing down, and she could tell he was using every bit of strength to finish what he needed to tell her.

"I love you, Margaret." He reached out to touch her, and Margaret took his hand in her own.

"And I love you," Margaret declared.

"Kiss me… one last time," he choked out.

Margaret leaned down and pressed her lips to his. She lingered there for several moments before she realized that he was gone.

"No, no, no, no, Michel, please do not leave me! Please, do not go!" She placed her head on his chest as huge sobs racked through her body. The man who had broken through her defenses and helped her find a way to love again was dead.

Everyone she loved, the Duke of Witherton killed. He may have not killed him the moment he pushed his sword into Michel's shoulder, but it caused the infection that took his life just the same.

What was she going to do? She knew she needed to do something, but she could not make herself stand up from beside Michel's bed.

God, give me the strength to get through this. I need you right now because I feel like I am going to break into a million pieces without Michel. I need your power to strengthen me and help me.

Margaret exited the room. Outside, her brother, Randall, his wife and Margaret's best friend, Jackie, along with Michel's brother, Monte were waiting.

"Is he gone?" Monte asked with a concerned look on his face.

Swallowing several times before she answered, she pushed out, "He is."

Stepping forward, Monte yelled at her, "This is your fault. You did this to him."

She flinched under the admonishment. She wanted to refute what he said, but part of her knew it to be true. If Michel had never met her, he would still be alive.

"What is that in your hand?" Monte demanded, grabbing the envelope from her. He tore it open and scanned the documents.

"What is the meaning of this? Did you talk him into doing this?" Monte accused, shaking the documents at her.

"I have no idea what you are talking about," Margaret defended.

"Although he left me his title, the Marquis de Badour, he left the rest of the family fortune to you! He has only been married to you a few days, and yet this new will materializes out of no where. You made him change it; I just know it," Monte spit out.

"It is not so. I did not even know he would do such a thing."

Randall yanked the papers from Monte's hands. He flipped to the last page, and after examining it, he explained, "He signed them over a month ago and had them take affect once he married my sister." After scanning through the rest, he added, "There is a clause that a portion of the fortune is to be set aside for the care of a Lady Marie Robineau." Randall eyebrows came together in confusion. "Who is that?"

"She's our sister," Monte asserted, "and far more entitled to the Robineau fortune than your sister."

"He also left a portion to you, Monte," Randall further explained. "It seems he wanted all of the people he cared for to be taken care of."

"This won't stand. I am having my lawyers look into this, so they can overturn this fraudulent document." As Monte stormed towards the exit, he tossed over his shoulder, "I will not let some foreign, money-seeking, harpy steal the family fortune out from under me."

Though she knew the fortune Michel left her in his will was his parting gift to her, she also knew that Monte would not rest until he kept her from it. She could feel in the pit of her stomach, it was not going to go her way, but she did not care. No amount of money would make up for her loss.

"Everything is packed, but Maggie, another ship does not depart for America until three days' time," Randall stated with worry in his voice.

"I know, so we need to go by carriage to the nearest port that has a ship leaving immediately."

"I will go find out the schedule for surrounding ports," Jackie said and quietly slipped out of the room.

"You're sure this is what you want to do?" Randall asked.

"Yes, but you and Jackie do not need to come with us."

"Do not be silly. You and Henry are our family," Randall stated. "I cannot imagine letting you slip away to America and never knowing where you are, or whether or not you are safe."

"Thank you, Rand, your loyalty means the world to me."

"I am sorry, Maggie, for what has happened over the past week. It is unfair, these turn of events."

Margaret nodded as she thought about what had happened. Monte had succeeded in overturning the will of her late husband, claiming the wedding was not legal since they had been unable to consummate the marriage.

The first night, they had both been exhausted and she did not want to further hurt his arm which was mending. The next day, the infection set in, rendering everything beyond helping Michel trivial.

Added to the turmoil surrounding her husband's death, there was the threat that the Duke of Witherton still posed.

Mulchere, her private investigator, had reported to her that Witherton was recovering in a nearby estate he owned, but it was only a matter of time before he recovered well enough to come after her again.

"I made the mistake of thinking I could stay here and Michel would be able to protect us. Perhaps if he had lived, that might have been the case, but now we will never know. It seems when it comes to Witherton, the only choice I have is to run."

"You did not know what was going to happen."

"You are right, but Michel is dead and it is because of my past catching up with me. I will not make that same mistake again. When we get to America, I am going to bury my past once and for all. Are you sure you are ready to walk away from our titles and life here?"

"You are my family, Mags, and wherever you go, I go. I lived without a title for almost half my life. This will be nothing new for me."

"Thank you, Rand. I do not know if I could do this without you."

"I will always be there for you, so you will never have to worry about that."

Margaret was standing in front of a ship again. Two days later and three towns away, she was about to set voyage and finally leave her past behind. Her heart ached for the two men she loved and lost. Both died under different circumstances, but the cause of their deaths came from one common factor: Witherton. She hated him for what he had taken from her—first her trust, then her reputation, and finally the loves of her life.

But a miracle happened the day after Michel passed away. When Margaret went up to get her son ready for their one-way trip to America, she found him sleeping. She looked at him and realized that not all was lost. He had gotten her through the death of her first husband, and he would help get her through the death of Michel.

God had given her this perfect miracle in the form of her son, and she gathered him in her arms and walked over to the window. She looked out that window and saw a mother bird rebuilding a nest that had been destroyed by a windstorm. She realized that she needed to be like that mother bird and rebuild her own life. She needed to be strong so she could take care of her family. And in order to find that strength, she needed to rely on God, because it was her faith that was going to get her through this season of loss.

And for the first time since she could remember, she felt true hope. Hope for a future that was unrestricted from the shackles of her past. Hope that she could build a life for her family that had meaning and was free from fear. Hope that what had been done to her would not define her. Hope was the gift God gave her in her darkest hour.

"Are you ready?" Randall asked, bringing Margaret back to the present.

Margaret turned to look at her twin and replied, "Yes. It is time for us to start our new life."

"Mon chéri, we have each other," Jackie declared, "and that is all that matters."

Margaret hugged her best friend. "I am glad you decided to still come with us."

"You have always been like family to me, and once I married Randy, we actually became family. I want to be wherever the both of you are," Jackie said with a loving smile.

Margaret's son ran up to her, grabbed her hand, and asked, "Bye-bye time, Mummy?"

She smiled down at her son and replied, "Yes, my darling, it is time for us to go make our new home."

"Michel with us?" Henry asked with hopeful expectation.

Margaret flinched inwardly due to the pain still being fresh from his death. She tried to hide her reaction by making herself hold the smile. "He is not going to be able to come with us, Henry."

"Oh," he said in a saddened tone, hanging his head in disappointment.

Margaret put her hand under her son's chin and raised it up so she could look him in the eyes. "It is going to be all right. He loved you very much, and I wish he could be with us, but he cannot. I love you, and Uncle Rand loves you, and Aunt Ja-Ja loves you. We are all going to be happy when we get to America."

Albert walked up to them and said, "Ma'am, it is time for us to board the ship now." Margaret nodded in acknowledgment, turned around to take one last look at France, and headed up the gangplank.

CHAPTER 1

1865 Port of New York, America

Margaret Learingam held on to the ship's rail with one hand and her toddler son with the other. As her family approached the New England shoreline, fear filled the pit of her stomach. Forced to flee to America, Margaret had no experience outside of Europe, where she had grown up in England and spent a year in France. She left everything behind, including her last name and titles, to keep her family safe. And now, in just a few moments, she would be stepping foot into a new world that held the potential to offer her and her family a way to stay alive and together.

Still haunted by the painful memories of losing the two men she loved, Margaret could not help but feel guilt over their deaths. Both her husbands were killed by the invidious Duke of Witherton, the man that forced her to flee to America.

The trip across the Atlantic Ocean had been long and grueling, as they had encountered several storms in the process, lengthening their journey and causing sickness to run rampant on board. In addition, due to Margaret's appearance, she had been receiving constant unsolicited attention from the single men on the ship, which made her uncomfortable. Her dark violet eyes and long raven locks contrasted against her smooth white skin, and her petite frame had adjusted admirably after childbirth. But she knew her aristocratic features were not going to be able to save her when they reached the new land. In fact, she had the type of appearance that could get her into trouble.

Fortunately, she had a brother who gave up his life in France to keep her safe. Randall was her twin and, in some ways, the most important person in her life. Margaret had gone to France to search for him after he had been lost at sea eight years prior. The twins' physical features were similar in almost every way, but it was where their identical-ness ended. Randall was outspoken and a reformed philanderer, while Margaret was more reserved.

Accompanying them was Jacquelyn, or Jackie, as her family called her. She would argue that she alone could claim to be Margaret's closest confidant. She was also Randall's newlywed wife. Jackie was a fiery strawberry blonde with golden-green eyes, whose second nature was to use her voluptuous body and personality to her benefit. Margaret still marveled at how their relationship was the catalyst for both of them to change their noncommittal ways. They made a fierce partnership.

Two loyal servants, Margaret's elderly butler, Albert, and personal servant, Sarah, chose to come with them. They were like family and had no ties to keep them in Europe. Together, all of them were going to forge a new life in the Colorado Territory with the land Margaret's deceased father secretly left her.

Many people had done it before them, had left their homes and lives behind to escape the law, poverty, or oppression. But she was fleeing to the new frontier in hopes of finding a place she could hide and never be found. Once and for all, she was going to leave behind all the horrible things that had happened to her in Europe.

During their oceanic journey, something amazing happened to Margaret's family. They met a preacher and his wife who were moving to America and wanted to start a church out west. And since the boat was mostly filled with young, unwed men moving to America to make quick and easy money, Pastor Nathan Thompson and his wife, Laura, decided it would be best to eat and socialize with Margaret and her family. Through their talks with them, Randall and Jackie came to know God, something Margaret had been praying for since she met Jackie and found Randall.

Margaret had accepted the Lord as her savior a couple years prior and wanted nothing more than to have the rest of her family feel the love, peace, and acceptance God offered. As Margaret watched the transformation in Randall and Jackie, it was incredible to see the changes in their lives. They hungered to read the Bible, to ask Pastor Thompson questions about God, and to embrace everything entailing being a Christian. Margaret was pleased and excited as she realized that their entire family was truly starting a new life as they approached the New World. As an added bonus, Randall and Jackie's thirst to learn more about God kindled Margaret's faith in a new way, giving her a desire to become close to God like never before.

With an appreciative smile, Margaret gazed intently at the approaching shoreline. This was going to be the start of their adventure to find their new home.

"Look at those docks. It is disgusting how they keep them. I cannot believe I followed you here."

Rolling her eyes, Margaret listened to her brother go on about how primitive the New World seemed to be. Personally, she found it fascinating. It was going to be so different than Europe. She had heard no one really paid attention to a person's class or their station in life here. It was as if everyone was equal. It was disturbing while intriguing.

"Oh, Rand, sometimes you are such a baby. You should be excited, like I am, about all the possibilities that this new place holds for us. Do you realize that here there are no titles or nobility? We are just like everyone else."

"You forget I only came into my title a few months ago. I barely got to use mine before I gave it up."

As they made their way down the gangplank, Jackie said, "Margaret is right, Randy. This place has charm." Jackie sniffed in distaste as a cart carrying dead fish was pulled by them. "Even if it is masked by repugnant, disagreeable bits and pieces."

"Well, Mags, what do we do from here?"

"Yes, Maggie"—Jackie had picked up Randall's habit of calling her by the nickname—"what is on the agenda?" she said in her noticeably thick French accent.

Margaret opened her parasol and placed it on her shoulder, saying, "We are going to get the supplies and men we need in order to join the wagons going west to the Colorado Territory."

"All right, but how are we going to afford that? Have you forgotten that we have no money?"

"I have a little bit left from what I saved up in France, and I have this." She pulled out the key that she had placed around her neck and hidden under her dress.

"Fetching necklace, my lovely sister, but what will *that* get us?"

She smiled slyly. "A few men who are willing to take the risk to see what is in our safety deposit box in Boulder."

"You have a safety deposit box there? How?"

"Father left it to me along with the deed to our land and new home."

"Well, what is in it?"

Margaret shrugged. "I have no idea, but no one else knows that."

"We are going to promise American profiteers, who are just looking for an excuse to shoot up anything or anyone, money that we do not even know we have? I think the heat has gotten to you, because that is completely insane."

She tensed her lips. "No, it is completely brilliant. If nothing else, we can sell some of my dresses and jewelry in order to pay them."

He frowned. "You do not have any left. You sold the majority of your possessions to pay for our passage over here, as did we all."

"I still have Charlie." She thought of her expensive and precious mare that she had raised since she was a colt. The thought of selling Charlotte's Pride made her inwardly cringe, since she had staked her plans for a horse ranch in Boulder on the mare. "She could fetch a nice sum, I think."

Glancing down at her left hand, Margaret looked at the engagement ring her fiancé, Michel, had given her, then over at her other hand where she wore her wedding ring from Henry. "And I have my rings. They should help enough to get us to Colorado."

Randall shook his head. "No, I will not let it come to that. You will never have to part with your rings or your horse. It is all you have left. Not over my dead body."

"Then we have to go with my idea." She looked up from staring at her hands. "Besides, admit it. What really bothers you is that I came up with the plan, not you. You have always been the one to get us out of a tough spot, and it hurts your pride that I am going to do it this time."

"No, that is not it. I only—"

Tucking a piece of her curly strawberry blonde hair behind her ear, Jackie interrupted their argument. "All right siblings, quit squabbling. I think we need to move on now." She turned to Randall and said, "Unless you have a better idea, I suggest you be quiet. Now, let us go find a way to barter for our supplies."

As they made their way down the docks, Randall decided the best place to recruit men for their expedition would be at the nearest tavern.

"We are only going to have one shot at this, so let me do the talking. They will receive everything better from a man, and they will probably feel more comfortable striking a deal with me."

Biting back her sharp reply that she was as good as any man and it was her money that he would be bargaining with, Margaret opted to say nothing instead. Even though she hated to admit it, it was true that Yankee men would receive the offer better from him. In the end, it might be the deciding factor.

"As you wish, Rand. But please, do not do anything that will compromise our position."

He winked at her. "I would not dream of it."

Margaret said a silent prayer. *Lord, please help my brother not to wreck our chances at gaining the help we need to reach the Colorado Territory. He has a way of making things more difficult than they need to be, so please help him to handle this situation in a productive manner.*

How did things come to this? Margaret was standing in a Yankee tavern surrounded by harlots and scoundrels, and her own brother had deserted her in order to gamble away the last of their money.

She winced as she saw Randall lose another hand. No wonder her brother had owed so much money to so many hooligans back in France. He was a horrible poker player. Margaret, who was a woman and had played the game only a handful of times in her youth, could have had a better chance at winning than her brother.

Exasperated, Margaret sighed heavily. What were they going to do? If he lost all their money, which it seemed he was bound and determine to do, then they were going to be worse off than they already were. It was time for her to intervene.

Margaret walked over from where she quietly had been watching to stand behind her brother. She put her hand on his shoulder and whispered firmly, "Rand, I think we should address the issue as to why we came in here."

Leaning his head back, Randall glanced at his sister. He then returned his attention back to his hand. "Maggie, dear, I think that our luck is about to change."

She glanced at his cards and frowned in puzzlement. It had been such a long time since she had played cards. She had been seven and the stable boy had been teaching her how to play five-card draw. At least, until her tutor found out and put an end to it, saying it was "improper" for a well-bred young lady to play games of chance.

Struggling to remember what beat what, she knew that four of anything was good, as well as sequenced numbers, especially if they were all the same color. But all her brother had was two pairs, both not being high numbers. She was quite sure that her brother did not possess a winning hand. She had to help him.

Margaret stared at her brother's cards and raised her eyebrows as if she were pleased with what she saw. Then she asked with an innocent voice, "Rand, are two kings and three queens good?"

There were murmurs around the table followed by several curses and shouts of anger. Then Margaret watched as four piles of cards were dropped to the table. They had all folded.

Randall smirked as he raked in the money that his sister had just helped him win. He stood up and grinned at the other men at the table. "I think we will take our leave from you."

Holding the newly acquired bag of American gold coins in his hand, Randall turned around and started to walk away, but a hand grabbed his arm before they could make their escape.

"Not with my money, you're not. You suckered us, boy, and that little gal of yours helped. I'm thinkin' I'm goin' to take my money back and then take out my anger on the both of ya."

Margaret watched as Randall tensed for a fight. She had not expected these rough Americans to take defeat so poorly. Poker could have only one winner, and tonight was not their night.

But now, it seemed her brother had won at the most inopportune time with a group that did not seem to take to outsiders, especially ones that beat them "at their own game" and took their money.

"I am sorry that you lost, but I need this money just as much as you do, if not more. Now, I will be leaving with both my money and the lady." Gradually, he pulled his arm free from the other man's grasp and pulled at the bottom of his jacket. "If you will excuse us, we must be on our way."

He turned and held out his arm for Margaret, but before she knew what was happening, she felt her brother fall away. She looked to the side and saw her brother grabbing his head. Someone must have hit him.

Randall quickly regained his balance and turned around, holding up his arms in defense. Margaret knew her brother was not about to go down without a fight. He would not want to be known for being taken down by a bunch of crazy Yanks.

He swung quick and hard, and the crack of his fist connecting with the other man's jaw resounded throughout the overcrowded tavern. The man staggered back but quickly recovered, showing he most probably had been in drunken poker fights before.

Just as the loudmouthed Yank pulled back to take

another swing, a voice interrupted the fight. "Bobby Budley, quit fightin' with the new fella. He won that money fair an' square an' ya know it. Let 'em be."

Bobby shuffled his feet, spit on the ground between them, and glared at Randall several seconds before stepping back. "Yer lucky that Johnny took a liken to ya, 'cause if he hadn't...." He let the thought finish itself. Everyone knew what he meant.

Randall wiped his brow with relief and turned around to face the man who had most probably saved their lives.

A burly man with shaggy brown hair and brown eyes, who looked like he had seen better times, greeted him. He smiled, showing a mouth with several teeth missing and an ugly gash that jaunted across his cheek.

"Name's Johnny Goodrich, an' I heard that yer looking fer a guide to the Colorado terr'tory. Seems lot o' people been wantin' to go there to get in on the s'posed 'Silver Rush.' Ya foreigners goin' fer that?"

"Yes, we need to go to Boulder, but not for the...," Randall answered, pausing awkwardly at the unknown phrase, "'Silver Rush.' We have some land there. Are you interested in taking the position as our head scout?"

The old Yank scratched his straggly beard and said, "'Pends."

"On what?"

"On how much ya payin'."

"Enough to make you exceedingly happy."

"How much might'n that be?"

"If you can get me a half dozen men, two wagons, oxen to pull the wagons, two additional horses and supplies, I will give you the winnings I just won."

The other man snorted and kicked the dust on the ground.

"That ain't enough to cover what me an' the boys cost, let alone supplies too."

"That, my fine fellow, is only a down payment. You will receive the rest when we all reach Boulder safely. And I can purchase the supplies, I suppose. Those winnings will be the down payment for 'you and the boys.' How does that sound?"

When Johnny frowned, Margaret started to worry until a smile crept across his face. "Now that sounds like a deal, partner. Be ready to move out in three days' time." He started to walk away, then turned back around. "Oh, an' be prepared for a heckuva trip. I hear the Cheyenne are on the warpath and are killin' up and down the Oregon Trail. It's gonna be a doozy of a time."

Margaret cautiously looked Johnny up and down, noting he did not look like one of the American cowboys she had heard about, but rather just the opposite. His round belly was an indication that he was extremely out of shape, which made her wonder how he had any chance of protecting them from highwaymen, much less Indians. But then, they did not have much choice in who to hire. They would have to take what they could get. She began to pray immediately. *God, please place a hedge of protection around us. We need you to keep us shielded during the long journey ahead. Only you can guard and keep us safe.*

Looking at her brother, Margaret saw her own worry reflected back in his matching violet eyes. Their faith in God would surely be tested in the months to come.

CHAPTER 2

Two days later, they were finally on the Oregon Trail, traveling to the Colorado Territory. Margaret could hardly believe it. The whole thing seemed so surreal. They were pushing into the unknown to claim land that they had never laid eyes on, and their whole future depended on it. Additionally, they were placing their lives in the hands of wild, uncultivated Yanks who could lead them, quite literally, into death as easily as to their new home.

Pastor Nathan Thompson and his wife asked to join their traveling party, as they felt led by God to travel to Boulder to start their new church. Including them, their party consisted of two dozen people.

Pressing her lips together as anxiety threatened to take over, Margaret glanced over her shoulder into the back of the wagon at her sleeping son. He was growing so fast and reminded her so much of her beloved Henry. She missed him terribly, and even though nearly four years had passed since he was killed, the pain from the past and how everything happened still bothered her.

Suddenly, Margaret was jolted out of the past by a loud screech in the distance. Putting her hand above her eyes, she scanned the terrain. In the distance, she saw a few vultures flying in circles. They must have found a carrion and were taking their turns eating.

The land was so different from her England. It was rough and dry, not like the moist, forestry home she grew up in. It was also completely opposite the cityscape of Paris. Yet, this new land held a certain appeal she could not quite understand or explain. It was as if something was pulling her forward.

The group had been traveling along the Oregon Trail for over five months. Their time on the trail had been lengthened considerably by a run of bad luck, to include losing several wheels, supplies being eaten by wild animals, and two hired men dying due to sickness. In addition, they had to wait out several rounds of unusual inclement weather conditions before proceeding. After all of their misfortunes along the journey, it was finally time for them to split off to the Overland Trail that would take them into the Colorado Territory.

Fall was fast approaching, and it was paramount that they reached Boulder before first snow. If they continued to make good time, they could be there within the next month.

Trotting up next to Margaret on his horse, Mister Goodrich shouted at her, "It's 'bout time to round up fer the ev'nin', miss. Why don't ya bring the wagon 'round an' we'll get dinner goin'."

"As you wish, Mister Goodrich."

He stared at her openly for a moment, leering at her curves and wagging his eyes, driving home his desire.

"I told you before, a good-lookin' gal like ya self needs a man out here. It ain't proper fer a single gal to be on the trail without one."

Margaret was uncomfortably aware how vulnerable she was being one of the only two single women in their group. The hired men were beginning to look at Sarah and her in ways she did not like. Neither of them wanted any part of the flirtations, which seemed to make their interest even greater, Mister Goodrich being at the front of the licentiousness pack.

Randall did his best to look out for her and Sarah, but he was only one man, and she worried what would happen if any of them got it into their heads to try to force their attention upon one of them.

Bringing the wagon to a stop, Margaret stated, "I am fine, Mister Goodrich, and I would appreciate it if you would not broach the subject again."

He started to turn away but decided against it. Angrily,

he barked out at her, "Ya think yer too good for us, Miss High-and-mighty. I'll have ya know that I could humble ya real quick now. An' b'sides what ya might think, ya ain't no better than us. If ya were, ya wouldn't be needin' us to lead ya an' ya never would've been here in the first place."

Ruffled because his accusation stung, Margaret squirmed in her seat on the driving bench of the wagon. She realized that he was partially correct. She no longer was a part of the society in which she had been raised. She could not use her title for fear that someone would end up telling the wrong person. She had even gone to the lengths of changing the family's last name to their maternal grandmother's maiden name to avoid any connection to their past. Yet, her title and name were what set her apart from these dirty Yanks. Without it, she was just like them.

She did not want to put herself in the same class as them, but if she alienated them, she could end up without a guide and be left to fend for herself in the merciless frontier land. If that happened, none of them would survive.

Hopefully, an apology would suffice Mister Goodrich. "I meant nothing by it but—"

Without any warning, the lecher leaned over and forced his mouth on hers. His putrid breath was revolting, and Margaret immediately felt bile rise in her throat in reaction. Quickly, she yanked away as her hand automatically flew out and slapped him soundly across the cheek.

Out of breath, she whispered in a hoarse voice, "Mister Goodrich, I would advise you to *never* touch me again."

He glared at her several seconds before turning and riding away, shouting over his shoulder, "This is far from o'er. Ya'll pay fer what ya just did."

As she watched him head toward the river, she felt an uneasy feeling in the pit of her stomach. Margaret began to shake uncontrollably. The forced affection brought back painful memories from her past that she had been trying to escape.

Margaret looked up to see Jackie and Sarah walking towards her. They came to a stop next to the wagon, as Jackie asked, "What just happened between you and our guide?"

Pulling a handkerchief from the pocket of her riding skirt, Margaret indignantly wiped Johnny's saliva from her mouth. She hopped down from the wagon and proceeded to walk around to the back, without answering her sister-in-law. But Jackie was persistent and followed her, saying, "You are not answering me, chéri. Perhaps you do not trust me as much as you say?"

"Nothing happened. It was just a misunderstanding," Margaret asserted.

"So you say, but I did not know one received a slap over 'nothing.' But then I am not used to your silly English customs. Hardly anything you do makes sense to we French. You are so backward in almost every way, perchance you *would* slap him over a misunderstanding." Jackie gave Margaret a sly smile and said flippantly, "I think I will go ask Randy about it. Maybe he can explain what happened.

After all, he is English, and perhaps he can explain it to a confused Frenchwoman."

Jackie turned around and grabbed the reins of one of the horses tied to the wagon. Margaret moved over and stood between Jackie and the horse, blocking Jackie from leaving.

"Please, do not mention this to Rand. It is unimportant, and he would only get mad and cause a scene. Then we would lose our guide, and it is not worth it. It is over and it will not happen again. I assure you."

"*What* will not happen again?"

Sighing, Margaret finally told Jackie what happened. "Mister Goodrich mistook my attempt at apologizing for offending him as a sign that I might be interested in his attention. I politely told him that I was not, and he did not receive it well. He overstepped his boundaries as our guide, and I put him in his place. He will not make that mistake again."

"How did he overstep?"

Margaret was irritated that Jackie was insisting on details she did not wish to discuss. With a clipped tone, she answered the question. "He forced a kiss on me, and I slapped him for his audacity, then warned him to never touch me again."

Jackie raised her eyebrows in surprise and laughed. "I guess that means our Mister Goodrich will not be bothering you again. Never mind him. He is just a leering old man who does not know his place." Jackie narrowed her eyes and pursed her lips together in frustration. "I have a good mind to tell Randy, just so he will put a stop to it. Do you know that he was boorish enough to voice his sordid attentions for me the day we met, even though he knew I was married to Randy? He deserves to be punished for his lack of respect. He needs to be reminded of his station."

Margaret nodded, pushing away her recently acknowledged fact that there was no difference between them and Mister Goodrich any longer. "You have a point, but I do not want to involve my brother. I think we should just forget the whole incident and put it behind us. Unfortunately, we need him to get to Boulder. Besides, I took care of it myself."

"It is too late not to involve me, Maggie." Jackie and Margaret jerked around to find Randall leaning against the corner of the wagon. "I have seen the way Mister Goodrich looks at you, and I have been meaning to… talk to him about it. But it seems this time he has crossed a line that cannot be overlooked. It needs to be addressed, and with what I just overheard my wife say, he has had it coming a long time."

"We didn't know you were here at camp. We thought you had gone to get water with the rest of the men."

"I was going to, but I came back because I forgot my knife. I got back just in time to catch the exchange between you and Mister Goodrich." Gripping his knife resolutely in his hand, Randall stated determinedly, "I am going to take care of this right now."

With that, he turned and headed toward the river to find their guide.

～

"I cannot believe that Rand punched Mister Goodrich," Margaret stated in disbelief. She had been shocked when Mister Goodrich walked back from the river with his hand on his face and a welt forming over his left eye.

"I cannot believe that Mister Goodrich decided to stay on after it happened."

"He is probably staying so he can get his money. *That* is the only thing that motivates *his* kind. He will not give up until he gets his share of our money in Boulder."

Jackie sniffed. "Yes, it is disappointing, but the men here are all the same. These Yanks are nothing but disgusting mongrels that would never know how to treat a woman, let alone a lady."

Margaret gave Jackie a crestfallen look. She was going to have no luck finding a good husband out here in the frontier. She told herself it was not a priority after all she had been through, but the idea of living without a partner for the rest of her life made her sad.

"I am sorry, mon chéri. I know you are without a husband and it must be difficult to think of the lack of potential out here."

"You are right, Jackie. The prospects are dismal, which means I need to learn to be self-reliant. Pinning all my hopes on marriage has never gotten me anywhere positive before. The last man I married died because of it. I do not think I want to go down that road again."

Margaret heard a commotion behind her and then felt a tap on her shoulder. She stood up and turned around to see her oldest friend and servant, Sarah, standing behind her, body full of tension.

"What is it Sarah?"

"My lady, Henry is calling for you. He has had another nightmare."

Jumping up from around the campfire, Margaret lifted her dirty skirts, and ran toward the wagon. Henry's nightmares were getting worse and more frequent. She had no idea why he was having them or what she could do to stop them.

She jumped into the back of the wagon and knelt beside her son. He was awake now and crying. Brushing his hair back from his sweaty forehead, Margaret whispered, "It is all right, Henry. Your mummy's here, and I am not leaving."

Sitting on the edge of his cot, she pulled her son into her arms.

"You are safe, and I will not let anything happen to you."

Margaret rocked him for several minutes as he slowly quieted. It scared her every time he woke up like this, and she continued to pray for the nightmares to stop. *Lord, please help Henry with these bad dreams he keeps having. I do not know where they come from, but you do. I ask you to free him from them and give him peaceful sleep.*

Sarah insisted that it was a natural thing and all children had bad dreams, but Margaret never remembered her or Rand ever having nightmares frequently. Deep down she worried the nightmares stemmed from him sensing the fear in her, which she tried desperately to keep hidden.

Often in the beginning, and even now on occasion, she would dream that her first husband was still alive and that they were together. In her dreams, she could still feel his touch and his love. And when he did not fill her dreams, Michel would visit her and they would be dancing at their wedding. He would whisper in her ear how much he loved her as he held her in his embrace. But when she would wake up, swearing she smelled one of their scents, she would reach out to touch them and only find emptiness. Feeling like she lost them all over again, she would curl into a ball and silently cry until morning came.

Other nights, her pleasant dreams were replaced by nightmares filled with the horror of the duke hunting her. She could feel his cold, angry grasp on her body, with his leering face near her as she screamed. She would try to free herself but be unable to escape. She would wake up in a thick sweat, panting with terror-filled tears.

In her worst gut-wrenching moments, it was her faith in God that sustained and helped her. Her faith allowed her to keep going and live for her son after the men she loved died. Her faith helped her find her brother, even when everyone else thought he was dead. Her faith brought her to this new world and continued to push her forward.

Looking down, Margaret smiled at her slumbering son. She cherished him more than anything in this world. God had blessed her with the perfect gift, a gift that gave her a reason to live every day, and a piece of her husband lived on through their child.

As she was quietly backing out of her wagon, a hand landed on her shoulder, causing her to jump. Then a voice said, "It is only me, Maggie."

Margaret relaxed. "What do you need, Rand?"

"I needed to let you know that a scout found Indian tracks just a little way off." When he frowned, Margaret knew he was worried. "And they are fresh. Hopefully, we will not run into them. But we have been hearing that the Cheyenne are on the warpath and in this area. If they do attack us, we need to be prepared. We are going to have a meeting right away. Be at the campfire in five minutes."

Margaret nodded and silently said a prayer that they would not have to carry out any plans they made that night. She shivered at the thought of what would happen to her family if they encountered Indians in such an isolated place.

CHAPTER 3

When the Indians attacked, it was just as the first rays of the sun burst forth across the meadow where the traveling party had made camp and prepared for battle. The small bands of settlers were tired from their long journey and lack of adequate sleep and food. The Indians had the superiority and took advantage.

The pandemonium of the situation overcame anything else. Margaret knew they were outnumbered, outgunned, and outsmarted. They were going to be slaughtered, and there was nothing they could do to stop it.

She crouched underneath the wagon, which had been turned upside down to protect the women and children, and watched in horror as, one by one, each of their men were killed. Margaret, along with Jackie and Henry, hid beneath one wagon, silently praying for the safety of their men, while Laura, Sarah and Albert were hidden beneath the other.

Clutching a gun, Margaret tried to help by firing through small holes in the wood of the wagon. She had little success, missing several times and only grazing one Indian warrior in the shoulder. The Indians were being methodical, slowly killing one man at a time. She was terrified of what would happen when they got to them.

Jackie was a wreck, witnessing her husband fend off attack after attack. Both women peeked through the small holes in the wood of the wagon. There were only two hired men left, as well as Mister Goodrich, Randall, and Pastor Thompson. Margaret bit her lip as she anxiously focused on the battle outside.

Randall was about to fire off another round at one of the Cheyenne warriors when his gun was knocked out of his hands by a tomahawk. Blood squirted from where the weapon had hit him, and Randall grabbed his hand in pain.

Margaret winced as she too felt the intense pain that was coursing through her twin. She wanted to shoot the Indian who relentlessly bore down on her brother, but she did not want to take the chance that she would hit Randall.

Glancing over at Jackie, Margaret noted how white her friend appeared. As long as she had known her, she had never seen such a stricken look on Jackie's face. Henry was curled in a ball with his eyes clenched shut and his hands over his ears. He hated all the screams and shouting going on outside the wagon.

Randall and the Indian were locked together in hand-to-hand combat, and Margaret knew her brother was at a disadvantage. It had been his right hand that had been wounded, so instead, he held his knife a bit awkwardly in his left.

He lunged and the light-footed Indian ducked away from the thrust. In return, the warrior distracted Randall by striking with one hand and knocking Randall's knife away with the other.

Randall dove for his knife, but the Indian kicked it away and then stepped on Randall's wounded hand to keep him from moving. When the Indian raised his tomahawk to strike, Margaret could stay hidden no longer.

Stumbling from underneath the wagon, she screamed like a madwoman. She could not lose her brother again. She raised the shotgun, supporting it under her other arm, and fired. The shot was dead-on and hit the Indian directly in the chest. The impact sent him sprawling on his back. He lay there unmoving, and when the rage that had enveloped Margaret began to fade, she realized that she had just taken another life. She had killed two men in her life, both in defense of her brother.

Numbed from her sudden insight, she had temporarily forgotten that she was standing in the middle of an Indian raid. It was not until she heard Randall yell, "Maggie, watch out behind you," that she remembered there was a battle going on around her.

She staggered around just in time to see an Indian rushing

at her but not in time to raise her shotgun. He knocked the weapon from her hands and grabbed her by the hair. When she struggled to get free, he pulled her hair so tight that she began to see spots. She clinched her eyes shut as she screamed out in pain. Tears rushed down her cheeks, not only from the pain but her fear as well. She opened her eyes to see the gleam of the Indian's tomahawk as he raised it into the air. In horror, she watched as the blade descended toward her.

Then from out of nowhere, she heard gunfire and saw the tomahawk fall from her enemy's hand. Reflexively, he let her go as he grabbed his wounded hand. A second shot followed and the Indian fell to the ground dead.

She let out a long breath that she did not realize she had been holding. Then quickly, she turned, picked up her shotgun, and ran to her brother's side. Randall wrapped a makeshift bandage from a handkerchief around his wounded hand as the siblings made their way over to one of the upside-down wagons, placing their backs to it.

Margaret stiffened as the battlefield became eerily quiet. Scanning the terrain, she was unable to ascertain the location of the Indians. Feeling their eyes on her, she was filled with dread, realizing they must be hiding because they were preparing for their final assault.

Putting her back toward her brother, Margaret raised her gun while they anxiously waited. "Rand, I am sorry I did not obey your orders, but I could not stay hidden and watch them kill you."

"Mags, I am not pleased that you went against my instructions, but I am grateful for your assistance," Randall stated.

"How is your hand? I nearly passed out when I saw the blood flow from the wound."

"It hurts profusely but it appears to be minor."

"I am glad to hear it. Do you know who took the shot that saved me? It sounded as if it came from the hills to the left, but none of our men are over there."

Randall frowned as he reloaded his gun. "I have no idea where it came from or who fired it."

"I owe whoever it is my life, Rand, and I want to thank whoever is responsible."

"You can thank me later," a deep, husky voice stated.

Brother and sister looked to their left, shocked to see a stranger approach on horseback. He skillfully dismounted from his horse while holding his rifle in his other hand. Taking a position beside the twins, he raised his gun to join them.

Within seconds of the stranger's arrival, a loud outpour of Indian war cries filled the meadow. Margaret forced herself to steady, not allowing terror to take hold of her body. She watched as the few remaining Indians charged their group in one huge rush.

The next few minutes were completely chaotic. Margaret was unable to keep track of anything but the Indians directly in front of her. She shot two of them, killing one and wounding another who retreated around the wagon.

It took the settlers several minutes of concentrated effort to force the determined Indians to flee. With a departing holler, one of the last Indians made a gesture and the remnants of their war party retreated.

When it was over, Margaret reached up with the outer layer of her simple brown skirt and wiped the sweat away from her face and hands before turning to face the stranger.

"I have not gotten to thank you properly, sir." She extended her hand, as she recently had been taught to do in the New World. "My name is Margaret Learingam, and this is my brother, Randall. I am indebted to you for intervening."

The stranger took her diminutive hand and shook it firmly in his own larger one. "My name is Cortland Westcott, and I am pleased to make your acquaintance, ma'am." He glanced at Randall and reached out his hand to him as well. "Pleased to meet you, mister."

Randall nodded. "And I, you, good sir."

Margaret took in Cortland Westcott's rugged good looks. He looked nothing like the other Yankee cowboys who were traveling with them. He was tall, standing a full head above her, with broad shoulders and a muscular build. His skin was thoroughly tan and his thick brown hair had sun-kissed blond tips, showing he must have worked outdoors a great deal of the time. His smile was refreshing; it was genuine and sincere, matching his stunning hazel eyes. Coupled with his manners and slight English accent, she deduced that, somewhere in his past, he had been educated in England and taught proper decorum.

He wore brown cotton trousers under leather chaps with a matching tan shirt and vest that molded to his body perfectly. For outwear, he wore a pair of boots with big-roweled spurs, a wide-brimmed hat, and a duster coat, all of which made him appear formidable and accustomed to the West.

Margaret had temporarily forgotten about Jackie until she heard her friend's voice say, "Randy, dear, I was positively a wreck as I watched you out there. Let me see your poor hand. Does it hurt much?"

Jackie had emerged from underneath the wagon, bringing Henry along with her, and rushed to Randall's side.

He put his arm around his wife and said, "It is fine. You need not worry, my darling."

Turning her attention to the stranger, Jackie asked, "Are you not going to introduce me to your new friend, chéri?"

Gesturing from her friend to Cortland, Margaret said, "Mister Westcott, may I introduce my sister-in-law, Missus Jacquelyn Learingam."

He nodded in Jackie's direction. "Pleased to meet you, ma'am."

Jackie smiled in a way that made her golden-green eyes sparkle with intrigue. "Thank you for your intercession, sir." To Margaret's amazement, he seemed indifferent to her.

Turning her attention back to her husband, Jackie said, "I do not know what I would have done, Randy, if something more severe had happened to you."

"We are all right and that is all that matters."

Margaret glanced down and felt a small hand grab her own. Cortland's attention was also on the small boy.

"Is that your son?" he asked the newly wedded couple.

Jackie snickered. "By no way, no. We were only married a little bit ago. He is Margaret's son."

Cortland's head snapped up and to the side, his eyes focused in surprise on the small boy's mother. "He's your son?"

"Yes, he is."

"Really? How old is he?"

"Almost three."

"Well, if he is to be of any use, he will have to pull his own weight."

Everyone stared at Cortland with disbelief. Randall shook his head. "I had no idea you Yanks were cruel enough to have small tykes work."

"Well, it is the way of things out here, after all. We need all the help we can get." Cortland was almost believable until he started to laugh and grinned. "I am only joking. I could not help it. You are all so serious."

Jackie and Randall started to laugh, and after a few moments, Margaret joined in, a bit awkwardly at first. But after a few more seconds, she began to relax and enjoy the laughter that none of them had felt in a long time.

Margaret turned to face the brawny cowboy, who still managed to carry himself with a boyish demeanor. She pulled her son in front of her and said, "May I introduce to you my son, Lor—" She paused, remembering not to place his title before his name. "—Henry Learingam."

Cortland tilted his head and narrowed his eyes in perplexity, but as suddenly as the confusion crossed his face, it disappeared. He got down on one knee and put out his hand to the young child. "My name is Cortland Westcott. I am honored to meet you, sir."

Henry studied him for several moments before reservedly shaking the cowboy's hand. He then blushed and quickly turned away, pushing his face into his mother's skirts.

"He is excessively shy around new people. He will get used to you soon enough."

Cortland stood up and brushed off his hands on his leather chaps. Smiling to herself, Margaret realized that she was curious about the cowboy. He was a strapping, good-looking man, who was also smart and charming, but she chastised herself for letting herself dwell on him. She had purposefully given up the idea of pursing a relationship with a man, knowing she could be content in surrounding herself with her family. She did not need a husband to complete her, and she could not bear to lose a third man she loved, which left no room for romance.

"What brought you out this way, Mister Westcott? Why were you good enough to help us fight off those savages?"

He winced and furrowed his eyebrows together in distaste. "Not all Indians are savages. They have a different way of life, but that does not make them animals."

She pressed her lips tightly shut and flushed with shame. She had become so used to hearing the other American men call Indians that, so it had become habit for her to call them by the same name. If she thought about it, she did not agree with the term "savages" either.

"I am sorry, you are right. That was improper of me. I hope that you will forgive my breach in manners."

"Of course, and as for the answer to your question, I came from the town of Boulder in the Colorado Territory. I was headed this way in order to take care of some business."

Margaret eyes grew round as she smiled with excitement. "That is where we are headed. We have land near there."

He smiled. "You don't say? We might be neighbors."

She looked around, realizing hardly anyone was left. "Where is everyone?"

Cortland frowned and shook his head. "I hate to tell you this, but it seems that the few remaining men you had fled when the older, burly one told them to get out." He made a quick glance around to assess the damage, then continued. "It seems they took the horses with them. I would not expect anything different from that type of men. I could tell from their demeanor that they were not men of honor."

Margaret realized the oxen that pulled the wagons were the only animals left, along with Charlie, who refused to allow anyone to ride her besides Margaret. She supposed she should be grateful the ruffians left them the ones they did, although she suspected the choice was made only due to not wanting to take the time to untie them from the overturned wagons where they had been secured prior to the battle. She sighed. "Mister Goodrich said I would pay for not accepting his offer. I suppose this must have been what he had in mind."

Randall put his arm around his sister. "It's all right, Mags. You did the right thing. That dirty old Yank was crooked from day one."

Cortland raised a brow in puzzlement. "What offer?"

"He made advances toward me and I turned him down."

Margaret watched as he shifted on his heels and glanced away. "You're not married?"

She shook her head. "My husband died a few years back."

"And you never remarried?"

She paused, still hurt from the loss of Michel. "I did, but my second husband passed away before we came to America." She gripped her hands together in front of her in frustration. "And now it seems we have no one to guide us to Boulder."

Margaret knew her tone made it evident she was hinting to see if he would take them. Cortland did not seem overly thrilled. He stared at her for several seconds, as if weighing his options. He shrugged. "If you are looking for a guide, I can take you the rest of the way to Boulder."

She smiled at him with gratitude. "Thank you. Your help is much appreciated. I do not know what we would do without your assistance."

"I think you would have fared far better than you give yourself credit. You seem to be well suited for frontier life. You were able to hold your own with a shotgun, even during an Indian attack."

"You are kind to think so, but all of this has been more difficult than I could have imagined."

"From your dust-covered appearance, you do not seem to mind getting your hands dirty. If you can tolerate that, everything else about this way of life can be learned."

Pastor Thompson, a thin, balding man, came running back from the bottom of the hills. Out of breath, he panted with his hands on his knees as he said, "I gave chase… to the hired men who absconded with our possessions… but they got away."

"Cortland Westcott, may I introduce Pastor Nathan Thompson."

The pastor straightened up and reached out his hand to shake Cortland's in return. "Pleased to meet you, sir. Thank you for coming to our defense. You most likely saved our lives."

"Of course, we all have to watch out for each other to make it in this place."

"Not all of us, it seems." The pastor gestured toward the hills where the hired men had fled during the attack.

"Where are you headed, Pastor Thompson?"

"To Boulder, where I plan to start a new church."

"Glad to hear it. Out of necessity, we have a makeshift church that meets in the schoolhouse, but the man who leads us, self-admittedly, is out of his depths."

"If you go to church, I can assume you are a God-fearing man?"

"Indeed. I have been a follower of Christ for a few years. My faith is the most important part of my life."

Cortland was a Christian too. Just one more quality to add to the already growing list of venerable attributes—and by Margaret's reckoning, the most important aspect of all.

"If you will excuse me a moment." Pastor Thompson made his way over to the second wagon, which was flipped over next to the one Margaret, Jackie, and Henry had been inside. He lifted the edge of the cloth and pulled his wife up from underneath. Sarah crawled out shortly after, followed by Alfred. Pastor Thompson escorted his wife over to the group. "Cortland Westcott, this is my wife, Laura Thompson."

Cortland nodded. "Pleased to meet you, ma'am."

"Thank you, good sir. We owe you a debt of gratitude for what you did."

"It was no bother. I am glad I could be of assistance."

Sarah arrived next. "These are our servants, Sarah and Alfred," Randall said.

Cortland dipped his head in their direction. "It is nice to meet you, ma'am, sir."

Both of them returned his greeting.

Margaret glanced around the area. "We need to bury all of the fallen men who died defending the group."

Cortland nodded. "I can take care of that."

"And I will help," Randall added.

"While we prepare the graves, the rest of you need to get the wagons turned back over and salvage as much of the supplies as possible. We need everything prepared to move as soon as we are done," Cortland stated.

Within an hour, the remaining settlers stood around freshly dug graves. Pastor Thompson spoke over the lifeless bodies of the fallen men. "We are grateful for the men who laid down their lives today to protect all of us. We knew the journey here would be difficult, but nothing prepares someone for this type of senseless loss. I did not know the other men well, but none of us will forget the ultimate sacrifice they made this day. Let us bow our heads as we pray to our heavenly father."

After the burial concluded, they went about finishing the preparations for their departure. As they put the last of the remaining undamaged supplies on the wagons, Cortland approached Margaret with a puzzled expression. "I was surprised to find out you had two servants in your traveling party. Not many settlers can afford to keep their servants on when coming to America. The only people I have known to do so have been nobility."

Margaret stiffened, realizing that it could be dangerous to have someone so clever poking around in her past. If she was not careful, he would unbury all her secrets. "They did not want to leave my service. I told them it would be hard and the pay minuscule, but they wanted to come nonetheless. It was their choice."

Cortland whistled sharply and a horse came trotting up, allowing him to grasp the reins. Margaret's eyes grew wide as she took in the beautiful piece of horseflesh that stood before her. During the commotion of the battle, she did not have time to notice Cortland's stallion, but now she took in his perfect lines and exceptional height, standing at least sixteen hands. He was striking with his light brown coat with white splotches and a thick white mane and tail.

She did not recognize any of the specific features, which made her wonder from which thoroughbred bloodline the horse came. "He is magnificent. Where did you get him?"

Smiling with pride, Cort stated, "I bred him from the parents of two sets of horses I got from an Irish settler and Indian trader."

Wanting to touch him, she stepped forward and stroked the stallion's neck. He neighed slightly in surprise but quickly relaxed.

Cortland watched Margaret with an appreciative look. "You seem comfortable around horses."

She glanced over at him and smiled. "I was raised around them, and my family bred them before I left Europe." Realizing she allowed her love for horses to override her etiquette, she stammered out, "Forgive me, I forgot to ask if it was all right for me to approach your horse." Quickly, she looked away in embarrassment.

"I have never minded a woman who knows what she wants and then takes it."

Margaret's eyes darted back to Cortland as she blushed from his forthright compliment. But secretly, she appreciated his unabashed approval. After a few more moments, she whistled softly. Obediently, Charlie trotted up to Margaret.

Cortland watched as the horse approached them, nodding in appreciation. "Is that mare one of the horses you raised?"

"Yes, my family bred her, and I have overseen her training since she was a foal."

"She's magnificent. What's her name?"

She hesitated a moment, then realized her horse would not be known in America. "Charlotte's Pride. I call her Charlie."

"I'm thoroughly impressed. She has excellent lines and a fine sheen to her coat. I never thought I would see the likes of her out here. I have seen my fair share of horses, since I'm constantly looking for new stock for my ranch just outside Boulder."

"You seem to know a significant amount about horses. How did you end up starting your ranch?"

While allowing the stallion to nuzzle his neck, Cortland said, "I love horses. Raising them was all I ever wanted to do. When I came over from Europe, I made it my ambition to start breeding and raising horses. Chester, here, is my pride and joy. I plan for him to be the start of a great American bloodline."

Margaret inhaled sharply. This was too much. Not only was this man incredibly good-looking, but it seemed he had the same passion for horses. His knowledge in the area made Margaret respect him. But as quickly as she allowed the hopeful feelings to emerge, she pushed them away, knowing she needed to tread lightly where this confident cowboy was concerned. She could not afford to get hurt again or let her family get harmed in the bargain.

Randall joined them and nodded. "You have a fine-looking horse there, Mister Westcott."

"Thank you. He's well-tempered as well. I daresay the best horse I have ever owned."

"If you do not mind my asking, what are you doing all the way out here?"

Margaret waited for a response, which did not come immediately. Several moments passed as she watched Cortland. He seemed distant, as if he were thinking of something ominous, and he had a troubled expression on his face. Finally, he looked up and said, "I was tracking the Indians that attacked your traveling party. They are wanted dead or alive for attacking a homestead in Boulder."

Before she could question him further about the incident in Boulder, Randall blurted, "I find it serendipitous we should meet you all the way out here, considering our family is planning on starting a horse farm on our land when we reach Boulder. Margaret plans to organize the breeding and training while I manage the business end of it. How fortunate, we will be breeding horses nearby one another."

"It will be nice to share similar endeavors as neighbors, but right now, we have to focus on the task at hand. We need to get on the road within the hour, in case any survivors of the raiding party decide to come back to finish what they started."

As the group finished fixing as much damage from the battle as they could, Margaret took Henry into the back of one of the wagons to get him ready for his morning nap, telling him a short story and singing him a song before he went to sleep.

Margaret thought about the budding possibilities she was beginning to see in regard to Cortland Westcott. Was it possible they had found an ally in the most unlikely of circumstances? Had God brought him into their lives for a purpose and, if so, what was it?

Detecting a murmur from Henry, Margaret looked down at her sleeping son. His little hand was resting in her own. She smiled as he shifted in his sleep, yet continued to hold tightly to her hand. Each day he was growing and settling more and more into his appearances. With his blond hair and brown eyes, he was looking more and more like her first husband.

From outside the wagon, her brother murmured, "Maggie, we need to be on our way."

She whispered back, "All right, Rand, I will be right out."

Gently removing her son's hand from her own, she laid it down beside him on the cot, then stood and leapt down from the backside of the wagon. Straightening her split skirt as she moved toward the driving bench, she hopped up and grabbed the reins to the oxen. The sun was already blazing above her head and she knew it was going to be a long day.

CHAPTER 4

They were getting close to the Colorado Territory. Excitement rose in the pit of her stomach, and she was not sure how long she was going to be able to contain it. Their new future was just over those mountains.

As they traveled, Margaret fought against her desire to get to know Cortland Westcott. He was the type of man she could easily find herself caring for deeply, which scared her. Watching him from a distance, she had learned, through his conversations around the nightly campfire, that he was a devoted Christian and attended church regularly in Boulder. His faith was also made evident by the way he conducted himself, showing kindness to everyone around him while being willing to help at every task. He was patient, always putting everyone else's needs before his own.

But even though she knew he was what she would want

in a partner, she avoided him at every opportunity. She did not want to take the chance of getting hurt again if something were to happen to him. They were in the wilderness, and it was a real possibility that he could be killed at any moment in this wild place. They had already been attacked by Indians, been deserted by their hired help, and lost a huge portion of their supplies, leaving them dangerously close to running out of food before they reached Boulder. She was afraid to get close to Cortland because every person she had ever cared for left or hurt her. She did not want to get involved with a gun-toting cowboy and have him do the same.

The sun was starting to descend and it was time to set up camp. Margaret brought the wagon to a stop and Sarah hoped out from the back, coming around to talk to her.

"Mistress, I am going to go fetch some water at the nearby river, if that is all right with you?"

"Yes, Sarah, thank you. How is Henry doing?"

Sarah shook her head. "Same as before, I'm afraid. He is resting now."

"I think I will check in on him for a moment before getting everything out for the evening meal."

Heading to the back of the wagon, Margaret climbed inside. She looked at her son, who was pale and had beads of sweat resting along his hairline and brows. The rugged conditions of the trip, along with the excessive heat, had taken their toll on everyone, but most harshly on her son. She had hoped he would start feeling well enough for her to be able to point out animals and types of formations they passed by, but his fatigue had dashed her desires for a majority of the journey. When she was not taking her turn driving the wagon, she was in the back trying to help her son feel better.

Today had proved to be a particular difficult time for Henry. After coaxing him to drink a few sips of water and placing a cool wet rag on his forehead, he fell back asleep.

Margaret began to pray. "Dear Lord, please help my son. He seems so weak, and you say in your word that when we are weak, you are strong. He needs your strength right now. Please help him to feel better."

Pulling out a canteen of water, she hopped down, found a spot in the shade, and leaned against the side of the wagon. She savored the feeling of the water sliding down her throat, knowing she probably would not get any more until evening since they were rationing the water.

Licking her lips, she scanned the area ahead of them. The mountains did not look too far off, but she had learned from experience on the trail to never assume anything. Looks could be deceiving, and from what she heard Cortland telling Randall, this was going to be the hardest part of the stretch.

She was still taking in her surroundings when she saw Cortland heading toward the nearby river. Just as he was about to enter the surrounding trees, Sarah came out with two large buckets in her hands. He said something that made Sarah laugh, and then she gave him a friendly smile.

He reached out and took the buckets from Sarah and they headed back to camp to join the others.

Margaret did not like the resentment she felt at seeing Cortland interact with Sarah. It unnerved her because it meant that, on some level, she already cared what he did and with whom he did it.

Trying to distract herself from her disconcerting feelings, Margaret rushed to the back of the wagon and roughly pulled out her last set of clean clothes, a bar of soap, and a fresh towel. Briskly, she marched toward the river.

When she reached the riverbank, she stared at the still, calm water for several seconds and was suddenly taken back to another time. She remembered when she and Henry had gone swimming together at their lake. It never failed that, whenever she was near a calm flow of water, she thought of that time. Reminiscing, she thought fondly of the time with her late husband. It had been so wonderful swimming with him there at their countryside estate in Brighton, not having a care in the world. It seemed like such a long time ago. She could not even remember how it felt to be carefree anymore. All she knew now was worry and fear. They consumed her, and no matter how hard she tried, she could not get free from the nagging fear that one day she would lose everything.

Sighing softly, she took off her outer clothes, stripping down to her undergarments. The anger the envy caused had dissipated and now was replaced by sadness. It was going to be a long time before she ever felt safe again.

Stepping into the water felt even better than the water she had just tasted. Finally, her body was able to cool down and begin to relax; the throbbing knots in her back were loosening up. It had been over a week since she had been able to take a bath. It was a luxury she had been warned none of them could afford with the Cheyenne still nearby. But needing to feel some sort of normalcy, she decided to take the chance, figuring a few relaxing moments in the water would far outweigh the risk. She wanted to feel like a woman again instead of a settler.

After washing her body and hair, she decided to stay in the comforting water for several more minutes. She leaned back and let her body float to the surface as she stared at the bright blue sky.

Just as she started to move toward the riverbank, she heard a noise behind her. Fearing the Indians were close, she swung around in the water, but instead, she found something equally alarming.

"Mister Goodrich, you startled me. I almost *screamed* with fright," she said, in a warning tone.

"I wouldn't if I was ya, missy."

Margaret swallowed the lump in her throat and then asked cautiously, "What are you doing here, sir?"

"I told the men to leave y'all, thinkin' my leavin' ya to the Injuns would be enough, but ya got out of that scrap with not a hair harmed on ya. That's when I 'cided it was time fer me to teach ya a lesson m'self. I'm goin' make ya pay fer makin' a fool of me."

Glancing around, Margaret realized she was trapped and vulnerable. Wearing only her shift, she felt completely bare under the water. The other bank of the river was too far away to make escape possible, and he blocked the side from which she entered. She had no options and they both knew it.

Biting her lip, she contemplated what to do. There had to be a way out. She inched as close to the edge of the bank as she dared while still remaining out of reach.

He grunted, rolling his burly shoulders with consideration. "If yer try to trick me, girl, I swear, I'll make ya pay once I get my hands on ya."

Margaret shivered with fright, knowing he meant his threat. He was the type of man who did not care for anyone but himself and took retaliation to excess.

Watching for her chance to escape, she kept her eyes locked on Johnny. She might only have one chance, and she was not about to let it slip past her.

After bending over to untie and remove his left shoe, he appeared fully focused on getting his right one off even quicker. The moment for escape was at hand. Darting quickly up and out of the water, Margaret scrambled past a shocked Johnny.

But hindered by her wet clothes, she was not quick enough. He turned around and, in two quick strides, yanked her to a stop by the shoulders. "Yer not gettin' away from me that easy, girl."

Swinging a closed fist, she used all her body weight as

leverage and heard a thud as her fist connected with his jawbone. Catching him off guard, she then hit him again in the nose. As he started to sway, Margaret stepped aside and let him fall face first into the ground.

Worried that he would get up at any moment, Margaret watched him closely as she grabbed her clothes and quickly pulled her top and skirt on. Not taking the time to put on her shoes, she picked them up, along with her towel and soap, and snuck past him. Just as she was about to reach the covering of the trees, she heard him move and mumble gruffly.

She glanced behind her and gasped as she saw the huge welt on the side of his cheek and the blood dripping from his nose. Not waiting for him to get up, Margaret darted behind one of the trees. She had to find a way to get back to camp.

"I know yer still 'round, missy, an' I aim to make ya pay for what ya just did. Nobody hits Johnny an' gets 'way with it."

Hearing him start to move, Margaret held her breath, hoping he would not come her way. Luck was on her side; as she peeked around the tree, she saw him head toward the left of where she stood.

Margaret prayed for protection. *Dear Lord, please help me get away from this despicable man. I need your protection during this dire time. Please, God, help me get back to camp without being harmed by Mister Goodrich.*

Glancing one last time, Margaret made sure he was in

fact going in the opposite direction, and started to run toward camp. But before she could break past the boundary of the trees, a hand grabbed her. Margaret trembled with terror as Johnny glared at her.

A voice boomed from the shadows of the trees, "I would let her go if I were you."

Margaret let out a sigh of relief. She was so glad that God had heard her prayers and sent Cortland to her rescue. She shuddered to think what would have happened if he had not.

Pulling free from the beastly man's grasp, she scrambled back to get as far away from him as possible.

Johnny spun around and growled. "Yer gonna regret interferin' with this, boy."

Cortland stepped into view and narrowed his eyes. "I think, by the end of this, you will be the one wishing you had not come back."

Cortland struck without any warning. He was quick and Johnny was not. The crack of Cortland's fist hitting him resounded through the area. He followed it with another punch and a blow to Johnny's stomach. Johnny tried to regain his balance, but Cortland was one step ahead of him. He grabbed the other man by the front of his shirt and pulled him off his feet. Glaring down into his eyes, Cortland said, "You coward, you ran out on them. Your petty retaliation nearly got my *fiancée* killed. If you ever come near her again, you will regret it."

Cortland released Johnny and the man crumpled to the

ground. Cortland stepped over him and walked to where Margaret was standing without looking back. He asked Margaret directly, "You ready to go?"

Still in shock from the whole incident, all she could do was nod. He took hold of her arm and guided her toward the camp.

Margaret's head was swimming in confusion. What had just happened? One moment, she was facing being ruined, and the next, Cortland was saving her again. Then, on top of all that, he had called her his fiancée. *Fiancée.* Why did he call her that?

Wanting answers to the questions rolling around in her head, Margaret asked, "Why did you call me your fiancée?"

"I figured, if he thought you were spoken for, he would not come after you again. It was for your own protection. Do not worry. I have no plans to stake my claim on you."

Gritting her teeth together in anger, she wondered how she could have been such a fool to believe he actually wanted her. After all, it was Sarah he often spent time talking to during the day, as well as at the evening campfires.

"I suppose with Sarah around, you would have no need for me."

Before he could respond, Margaret pulled free from his grasp and hurried toward her brother, who was standing by one of the wagons. As she dropped the items she was carrying, she placed her head on his chest as he wrapped his arms around her. Cortland walked up as Randall was comforting

Margaret. "Maggie, what is wrong? You are shaking," Randall asked.

Margaret said nothing, only allowing Randall to hold her. She was so worn by the whole horrible ordeal that she needed the comfort.

"Can you tell me what happened, Mags?" Randall asked.

Interjecting, Cort said, "Your old guide showed up and tried to take advantage of your sister. I made sure he will not be bothering her again."

Randall glanced over his shoulder at Cortland and smiled tensely. "I get the feeling I owe you another debt of gratitude. Thank you for interceding on my sister's behalf. It should have been me protecting her. If that rotten man had succeeded in…. I never would have forgiven myself. I am in debt to you. Whenever you need anything, let me now. I will not hesitate to help you."

Cortland nodded. "I am glad I chose to go down to get water for the horses at just the right time."

CHAPTER 5

As per usual, with his Bible in hand, Cortland approached Margaret as they sat around the morning campfire for breakfast. She had noticed that, before his morning meal, Cortland often had a Bible with him and would disappear for several minutes. It was one of the few periods of the day he did not remain with the group. She wondered what he was doing all alone. Was he spending time with God by praying and reading his Bible? She did the same every morning when she was in her wagon. Secretly, it made her even more attracted to Cortland. It was alluring, the idea of a man who was devoted to God so keenly.

He looked at Margaret, as if he were studying her, and after a few moments, he asked, "Would you like to go with me for a ride to scout out the trail going through the mountain pass, Missus Learingam?"

Trying to control her reaction, Margaret waited what seemed an appropriate amount of time. "I suppose I can have Sarah drive the wagon and go with you, Mister Westcott."

Cortland gave her a roguish grin. "Let's go, then."

Margaret had permanently started wearing a split riding skirt and button-up blouse for ease after a few weeks on the trail. She hated the nuisance of wearing a full dress, and all it entailed, while they were traveling. As Margaret mounted Charlie, she tried to hide her nervousness.

Several minutes later, she was stuck in the middle of the forest on a mountain miles away from anyone else besides him.

"I think we should stop for a moment and let the horses take a rest."

Margaret jerked slightly, startled out of her thoughts. Glancing at Cortland wearily, she replied, "If you think it best, Mister Westcott."

"I think we have been acquainted long enough for you to start calling me Cort."

"Then you must call me Margaret."

Cort jumped down from his horse and walked over to Margaret's side, reaching up to offer to help her down. She paused for a moment, looking at his extended hand suspiciously. But in the end, she put her hand in his.

As he helped her dismount, she slid down the length of

him. When he gently placed her on the ground, she looked up at him, their eyes locking for a flickering second. Then as quickly as it came, it passed and she pulled away.

Margaret sidestepped past Cort and moved to stand at the front side of her horse. Stroking Charlie's mane, she said, "I am glad that you asked me to come along with you, Cort. It has been some time since I have been able to take Charlie riding."

Charlie neighed and kicked at the dirt in response. Margaret laughed softly, adding, "Sounds like Charlie's missed riding as much as me."

"You are welcome, Margaret. I am glad that you agreed to come. It would have been lonely without you along."

Margaret glanced to where Cort was still standing.

She was curious to know his intention toward her. Did he want to be with her in any way, or was he merely passing time with her as they made their way to Boulder?

"Are you glad that I wanted to come?"

"Did you *want* to come?"

Turning to face him, she stared at him plainly for several seconds before replying, "Yes."

He stared back at her with the same intensity before bridging the gap between them. Margaret braced herself in anticipation of what was going to happen. When he reached down and took her cheek in his hand, she leaned into it, savoring the feel of his skin against her own. It felt so good to have him touch her. Wanting more, she moved forward and leaned against him, putting her hands delicately on his chest. He wrapped his arms around her and enfolded her in his embrace.

They stood there for several moments before Margaret looked up at him expectantly. "Are you going to kiss me?"

"Do you want me to kiss you, Margaret?"

Slowly, she nodded. Cort brushed a lock of hair out of her face, smiling down at her. Gradually, his lips descended until they met hers. The kiss was gentle, both of them testing, unsure.

Cort broke the kiss, pulling back he whispered, "I have wanted to kiss you for some time now."

"Why did it take you so long?"

"I wasn't sure if you felt the same."

Margaret averted her eyes. "I have to admit, I have confused feelings where you are concerned."

Reaching out, Cort touched the side of her cheek again. "What confuses you?"

"I am scared to care for a man again."

"You don't have to be afraid. I believe God brought us together for a reason."

"I just think it is best if we keep our distance."

A look of hurt crossed Cort's face before he looked away. "I will honor whatever you want." Cort lifted his hand to his forehead to shield his eyes as he scanned the terrain. "We should probably head back. It looks like there are some storm clouds on the horizon."

Margaret did not argue, realizing it was better this way. She hated all these mixed emotions she was feeling for Cort.

Part of her wanted to open her heart to him, but the other part was afraid because of her past. Rather than making a decision on what to do, she decided to return to aloofness when dealing with Cort until they reached Boulder. Then they could part ways, and she would be free to focus on starting over.

As they reached the wagons, Cort shouted out, "We need to stop here and make camp. A storm is heading this way."

Randall and Pastor Thompson quickly pulled the wagons to a halt. Everyone began scurrying around, preparing for the storm.

The men tied down the wagons and secured the oxen and two horses. The women made sure that all the supplies were covered and nothing would be damaged from winds or rain.

After all the chores were finished, Randall turned to Cort and offered, "Mister Westcott, you can join our family in our wagon during the storm if you wish."

His eyes darted skeptically to Margaret. "It might be best if I stay outside and keep an eye on the animals."

"Do you think that's safe?" Jackie inquired.

"It won't be the first time I've been outside during a storm." Cort assured.

Guilt flooded Margaret's heart. He was willing to stay

out in a dangerous situation to avoid being near her. She knew he was trying to honor her request.

Pastor Thompson must have noticed the awkwardness between Margaret and Cort because he offered a seat in his own wagon. "You are more than welcome to stay with us for the duration, Mister Westcott."

"Thank you kindly, Pastor, but I'll be fine." His eyes flickered to Margaret once more before he added, "I can use the time alone to pray on some matters. If it gets too bad, I'll take you up on your offer."

As raindrops started to fall, Margaret tilted her head up and let a few fall on her face before she turned around and headed to her wagon.

She had always liked the sound and smell of rain, but storms were a different story, especially out on the trail where there was minimal protection from the elements.

As she entered her wagon, Henry was sitting on the edge of one of the cots. His eyes were wide with fright and his lower lip was trembling.

She gathered him up into her arms. "It is all right, darling. Mummy is here."

"Where, Cort?"

Margaret's heart tightened at her son's question. When he was feeling up to be outside, Cort often played with Henry around the campfire, read to him from the Bible, or let him "comb" Chester. His interactions with her son was another reason Margaret was confused about Cort. He was so sweet with him, she knew he would be a good father.

"Cort is busy, darling. Whatever you need, I can do it."

Shaking his head adamantly, Henry demanded, "Want Cort."

Hesitantly, she thought about her options. She could ignore her son's request, but she knew if she did, she was doing it out of selfish motives. She could go ask Cort to come spend time with her son, but she had just decided to keep her distance to protect her heart. That would be doing just the opposite.

Deciding her son's feelings were more important than her own, she set Henry down as she said, "I will be right back with Cort."

Just as she was getting out of the wagon, Randall and Jackie were getting ready to get in.

"Where are you off to?" Randall asked with curiosity.

"Henry wants Cort to be with him. I am going to go see if he will be amicable to staying with us during the storm. Do you know where he decided to take shelter?"

"He's over by the horses, underneath a couple of trees."

Margaret nodded and headed off in that direction. She found Cort leaning against a set of boulders with his duster coat pulled in around him and his hat down over his face. Apparently, he was an expert at being out in the elements.

"Pardon me, Cort, but I was wondering if you mind coming to my wagon?" Margaret inquired. "Henry is asking for you."

Slowly, Cort raised his hand and pushed back his hat to

reveal his face. One eyebrow shot up as he looked at her through amused eyes.

"I thought you wanted me to keep my distance."

She stiffened as she crossed her arms. "I did, but this is not for me. It is for Henry."

Climbing to his feet, Cort adjusted his hat and coat. "For Henry then. He's a good boy and I don't want whatever happened between us to cause him to think I don't care."

Against her will, her heart filled with warmth at the kind regard Cort had for her son. All she had wanted since he was born, was to find a man worthy to be his father. Michel could have been, if he had been given the chance, but it was robbed from him by Witherton.

Perhaps Cort was right, and God had brought them together. He was a man that was good to her son and could provide a good life for them. Could that potential life be enough for her to open her heart and let him in?

As they started to make their way to the wagon, fighting against the wind, Margaret said, "Thank you for doing this."

"What was that? I can't hear you over the wind that's kicking up," Cort yelled.

Margaret stopped and turned to face Cort. Even in his disheveled appearance, he looked handsome. He was grinning at her, causing his eyes to sparkle. It was all she could do to not lean up and kiss him.

In a louder voice, she shouted, "I said, 'thank you.' I appreciate you doing this."

Huge gusts of wind whipped around them, causing Margaret's hair to twist and twirl. Cort reached out and gently pushed at several strands that were in her face. He tucked them behind her ear, then let his hand linger on the side of her face.

"It seems I'm not very good at keeping my distance when it comes to you," Cort confessed.

She felt him move towards her, and she knew from the smoldering look in his eyes, he planned to kiss her again. She should move away. She should turn away and head back to the wagon, but something kept her rooted to the spot.

The whistling of the wind was overwhelming, but she could swear the pounding in her chest was louder. She pressed her lips together as she waited for his lips to meet her own.

But before he could kiss her again, she heard him yell, "Watch out!"

Margaret felt Cort's arms wrap around her as he pulled her towards the Thompsons' wagon. Just as they arrived, he dove underneath with Margaret in his arms. Behind them, she heard a loud thud.

"What is going on?" Margaret asked in utter confusion.

He whispered against her ear, "A tree just got struck by lightning and fell. I could tell it was going to land where we were standing. I had to act quickly to keep you safe."

He had just saved her life again. Though she knew she

no longer needed to be in his arms, she found herself wanting to stay.

"I suppose I owe you another thank you."

"Any time," he said with another grin. "I enjoy rescuing you."

"I hope I will not be needing any more once I arrive in Boulder."

"I was thinking about when we arrive in Boulder. I don't like the idea of us keeping our distance."

"You don't?" Margaret asked, trying to focus on anything other than his lips that were only a few inches away.

"Just the opposite. You need a husband to protect and provide for you and Henry. I need a strong, good woman who is not afraid of frontier life. I think we should get married."

Her mouth went dry as her eyes grew round with shock. What did he just ask her?

"Margaret, I am asking you to marry me."

Keeping her eyes averted, she weighed out the different sides. If she agreed, her family would have a good provider and protection by a Christian man—everything she had been wanting for Henry. But somewhere between France and where she was now, she had come to a place where she wanted not only these things for her son, but she also wanted love for herself. She would rather be alone than subject herself to a loveless marriage. And though she knew that Cort cared about her well-being, she saw no signs that he loved her.

Margaret held back the tears and forced out, "I cannot marry you, Cort."

He furrowed his eyebrows together in disbelief. "But it is the smartest thing to do. Why won't you agree?"

"I cannot."

"We are mutually attracted to each other, and we have a growing friendship, both of which are a sturdy foundation for any relationship. Explain to me why it will not work."

Pushing him away, she blurted out, "Because I want more than that. I want more than you can offer."

She tried to climb out from under the wagon. Even though the storm was in full rage, she would rather brave it then stay close to him a moment longer.

But he grabbed her arm, stopping her from fleeing. "Margaret, you can't go out there. You might not want to stay here with me, but it's not safe out there."

"I can take care of myself," she said, yanking free from his grasp, and climbing out.

The moment the cold, wet rain slapped against her body, she knew she had acted rashly, but she did not care. She needed to escape and get back to Henry.

She pushed forward, trying to see through the pelting rain and wind. After a few minutes of slow and deliberate movements, she reached the other wagon and lifted the entry flap.

"Maggie, dear, we were starting to worry that you had

gotten lost. But then, you had Cort with you, and he knows the area quite well, does he not."

Margaret moved past Randall without answering him. She picked up Henry from Jackie's lap, trying to forget about what just happened between Cort and her.

"Are you all right, Maggie?" Jackie asked.

Margaret refused to glance up. "Yes."

"You seemed a bit ruffled from being outside, and not just from the storm. I also noticed Cort is not with you. Did something happen with him? Did the two of you have a fight?"

"You could say that," Margaret whispered.

"What happened?"

"He asked me to marry him—"

"Oh, that's wonderful, chéri!" Jackie interrupted.

"But I told him no."

"Why?"

"Because I do not think things would work out between us. We are completely different."

"I do not believe that. Look at Randy and me. We come from completely different pasts, but we are perfect together."

"Yes, but Rand also loves you dearly."

"Oh… so this is really about *love*. I should have guessed. Only two things can upset a woman so: one is love and the other is a woman more beautiful than herself. The latter is impossible with you, chéri." Jackie leaned forward and patted Margaret's knee. "Maggie, you must understand that love does not always operate the same. Yes, Rand and I did fall in love very quickly, and we were in love when we got married. But that is not the only way. Sometimes, love comes later. If you act out love, the feelings will follow. I have learned that from reading the Bible. Cort is a good man. He cares for you and the attraction is obvious. The rest will come in time."

Margaret slumped forward and put her face in her hands. She waited several moments before saying softly, "I cannot marry him without knowing he will love me. What if it does not come in time? I could not bear it."

"Then you were right to say no, and you must wait until you are certain. It is not the end of the world, and he will understand why you have not accepted. You did explain to him all of this, did you not?"

Looking up, Margaret brushed a tear away. "No, I just told him I could not."

"Oh, Maggie, you need to let him know what is going on. He will wait for you. I know this because I have seen the way he watches you. But if you leave it this way, you might miss out on the best thing in the Americas."

"Thank you for trying to help, Jackie, but I am going to have to handle this my way. It is best if I leave things the way they are. I do not want him to fake anything or try to convince me he is feeling something he does not." She pressed her lips together, pausing a moment, then added, "I would rather be alone than never know whether he genuinely loves me or not."

Jackie shook her head. "Do not pass up the chance at experiencing something wonderful because of fear, chéri." After a moment's hesitation, Jackie added softly, "I do not believe in fate. You know this because you have seen me make my own. But most importantly, now I rely on God. He wants to guide our lives, and I believe that He brought Cort into your life for a very specific and special reason. God loves you, Maggie, and He wants what is best for you. Do not throw away what He has given you."

She was shocked that her friend, who was a new Christian, just told her something that she as a Christian should have already known. It was embarrassing how little she really put her trust in God. It had been that way since she was a little child, so afraid to give up control to anyone, even to the one who made her.

Margaret replied in a saddened voice, "I know you are right, Jackie. I just do not see a way for Cort and me to be together."

CHAPTER 6

Several days passed while Margaret struggled to get her emotions under control. It was through her own stupidity that she allowed herself to care for a man who was only looking for a sturdy frontier wife, not love. And she knew, even though she could be what he wanted, she feared he could never be what she needed.

"Mama, why you cry?"

Margaret lifted her face from where it had been resting in her hands. She sniffed lightly and, after a few seconds, replied, "Nothing, darling, I only had something in my eye. It is gone now and it will not be coming back. I promise."

"You sad, Mama?"

"Why do you ask, Henry?"

"I like when you happy."

"Henry, darling, I think you should go back to sleep and

rest some more before dinnertime. You have not been feeling well, you know."

Margaret watched her son pout, sulking that he was not getting the answer he wished.

"But I—"

"No 'buts,' Henry. Go to sleep now. I do not want you getting sick again."

She was actually quite worried about her son. He had gotten sick twice since they started their trip from France and had been fatigued the entire duration. It continuously made her flash back to when he was only a few months old and almost died from pneumonia. She feared that he might not survive another attack of the fever.

When he bit his lip in anger, Margaret frowned at him and then tapped his cheek. "Do not bite your lip, Henry. It is a very naughty habit."

He started to object but saw the warning look on her face and opted to obey. "Yes, Mama."

"I will be back in a couple of hours to wake you."

They were back on the Overland Trail, and according to Cort's calculations, they would arrive in Boulder in two days. That meant she had to get through the next couple of days, and then she would be rid of him forever.

She hated his ability to affect her, even though she had tried to distance herself since she refused his proposal. Her heart pounded every time he looked at her, and she secretly wanted to feel his kiss on her lips again. But she would not return his look or let him know the effect he still had on her.

Margaret forced herself to be courageous. She was good at being alone. First, it had been out of necessity; now it was out of choice. If she were tied to no man, then no man could hurt her. And if that meant never feeling love again, so be it.

But that all changed in a flash, and nothing prepared her for her reaction. One moment, Cort was riding his horse, and the next, something hit him in his right shoulder hard enough to knock him off.

At first, Margaret thought they were under attack by the Cheyenne again and quickly halted the oxen pulling her wagon. She frantically looked around but could see nothing but their own party.

Without further thought, Margaret jumped down from the wagon and rushed to Cort's side, kneeling beside him.

He had landed face first but had rolled over to his back. Margaret reached out to see to his injury, but he grabbed her hand and pushed it away. "Don't. It's nothing."

"What happened?"

With narrowed eyes, he replied, "I think I know."

Realizing he was looking at something over her shoulder, she glanced up to see her brother standing behind her. He seemed overly undisturbed with what happened to their guide. Margaret clenched her teeth in irritation, recognizing that something was going on of which she was not aware.

With audible irritation, Cort said, "I think that you have accomplished your goal, Randall."

"Sorry, I figured it was the only sure way to get her attention."

Margaret looked around and saw a small rock nearby. It must have been what hit Cort in the shoulder. At least, it turned out, her brother still had as good an aim as he did when he was a child. If he had been slightly off, he might have hit Cort in the head, causing dire consequences.

Randall had a smirk on his face. "Glad to see no permanent damage was done."

"No thanks to you, friend," Cort retorted.

Glaring at her brother, Margaret recognized his ploy was an attempt to show her concern for Cort. Of course, any decent person would have responded the way she had, except she doubted anyone would have run with sheer fright while fighting back tears. With one simple deed, her own brother revealed how much she cared about Cort.

While starting to sit up, Cort groaned in pain.

"Are you all right?" Margaret couldn't mask her worry.

"Yes. I will be undeniably sore for the next few days, but I'll manage. We need to talk." He looked past Margaret and raised his eyes pointedly to Randall. "Alone."

"I can detect when I have overstayed my welcome. I am on my way."

Margaret stared at Cort and held her breath in anticipation. What was he thinking? She wondered if he knew how he affected her. It unnerved her how he stared at her in silence the way he often did.

Deciding to take a defensive stance, Margaret asked, "What do we need to discuss? Everything has been said that needs to be."

"Well, you may have nothing to say to me, but I do have something to tell you."

Trying to retreat with what little dignity she had left, Margaret began to stand up. Grabbing her arm and pulling her back down, Cort said forcefully, "Oh no, you don't."

"If you insist on intimidating me and forcing me to hear what you have to say, make it quick." Margaret glanced over his shoulder, trying to pretend she was disinterested.

"Yes, ma'am," he said teasingly, with a grin. Then an intent look came over him. "When I proposed to you, there was something I left out, Margaret."

Without being able to help it, her hopeful eyes darted to his as she waited for him to continue.

"Margaret, I love you. I asked you to marry me because you are the most beautiful, charming, and strong woman I have ever had the pleasure of knowing. Frankly, I want to know you will agree to be mine before we get to Boulder because I don't want any other man to even think about proposing to you."

Margaret was stunned. She never thought she would hear a confession like that from him. But she was still confused about one thing. "If what you say is true, why did you not say it when you proposed?"

He smiled and chuckled. "I was being practical. I was giving the logical reasons together, not realizing the most important reason was because I love you."

She stared at him in awe. In that moment, she knew she also loved him in return. This man was everything she had ever wanted.

"You do not know how much it means to me to hear you say you love me. I am glad you did not give up on me."

"I fight for what I want, Margaret. Maybe not always in the traditional sense. Sometimes, I do it on my knees. I can honestly say I earnestly sought Christ in prayer about us starting a relationship, and the Lord has given me His blessing. God has revealed to me that you are angry about some things that have happened in your past and that you even blame yourself for some of it, but He wants to help you heal your past wounds."

Margaret inhaled sharply; shocked at Cort's admission. She knew he was telling the truth because she had told no one about her feelings of guilt. "I must confess I am still young in my faith. I do not nearly have the relationship with God I wish I did."

"God plans to use our relationship to bring you closer to Him."

It was odd to hear someone speak about conversing with God as if it was as common as speaking with another person. Even after giving her life to the Lord, Margaret had never had that kind of relationship with God. She had been so preoccupied with all her plans and problems, she never took the time to go to church consistently or focus her time in prayer or the Bible the way she should. All of that was going to change, because she wanted to be the kind of wife Cort deserved.

Smiling across at the man God had brought into her life, the man who was beginning to mean more to her than anyone else in the world, she answered with the desire she had been covertly keeping hostage in her heart. "I will marry you, Cort Westcott."

CHAPTER 7

They arrived in Boulder at dusk. The buzz of a huge silver strike just outside of town had the whole place flooded with people looking to strike it rich. Everyone from paupers to what looked like nobility floated across the crowded streets.

Boulder was still a relatively new town, only being established in 1858 when a group of investors decided the location would be an ideal staging area for mining.

Her father had heard that land in the Colorado Territory might be a good investment and had purchased some from the investors in 1859, then added a homestead to make the property functional.

Her father's investment seemed to be one of the best decisions he could have made. It was going to make his son a very rich man.

The group was thrilled about the upcoming wedding, but at the moment, they were more excited to finally be back in civilization where they could have beds, baths, and clean clothes.

As Margaret enjoyed a hot bath in the hotel room she was renting until she and Cort were married, she reveled in the luxury she had not been able to experience in several months. Grateful everything was falling into place, she thought about how she had been worried nothing would work out between them. But there she was, about to become Cort's wife.

Margaret chose to wear the prettiest of the few gowns she had brought over from France. It was of the purest pink silk and trimmed with gold and pearls. With a fitted waist and bare shoulders, the dress was breathtaking.

"You look lovely tonight, Margaret." Cort took her hand in his, kissing the top softly before helping her into her chair inside the dining hall of the hotel. Without taking his admiring eyes off her, he made his way around the table to sit across from her.

Randall leaned over, saying from his seat next to her, "I must admit, sis, you look quite striking with that dress on."

"What about me, Randy? Are you not going to compliment your wife?"

Randall brought his attention to Jackie, who stood at the entrance of the room. "You look ravishing, my sweet, as always."

"You look tantalizing yourself, chéri."

Margaret was not embarrassed anymore when the two of them talked that way. In fact, she felt like blurting out the same things to Cort. Instead, she opted for a little more veiled comment, saying, "I think Cort can hold his own with my brother."

All eyes turned to Margaret, and a look of pleasure mixed with slight embarrassment crossed Cort's face. "Thank you. You flatter me too much."

She leaned across the table, replying with a smile, "I think not."

Bending forward to meet her, he brushed a kiss across her cheek, saying in her ear as he retreated, "I cannot wait until the week's end."

A blush stole across her cheeks. She too had been anticipating their wedding. They had decided to wait a week so that she could have a dress made and get everything settled. But a week was beginning to feel like forever.

Dinner went smoothly. It was nice to be able to have a refined meal with gentlemen and ladies again. An English couple, Lord and Lady York of Ashbury, had joined them for dinner. Also in attendance was Pastor Thompson and his wife. The food was delicious and the conversation delightful.

But the more Margaret thought about her upcoming commitment to Cort, she was puzzled by the fact that Cort did not seem to fit the typical American cowboy she had become accustomed to encountering along their trip west. Manners and decorum were two things that were surely lacking in the Americas, especially in the West, and Cort demonstrated both in abundance. She was dying to find out the secrets she knew he had buried inside.

Yet, it seemed hypocritical of her when she had her own secrets that she kept hidden. She wanted to tell Cort about her past, especially since he told her that God planned to use him to help her mend it, but she didn't know how. She was also worried that it would change how he saw her.

During dinner, Randall related that he had gone to the bank, and sure enough, the deed had been there along with several bags of silver. He believed that he and Jackie could do quite well with it, after giving Margaret her portion, which she planned to use to help with Cort's ranch.

After dinner, Cort cleared his throat, bringing the conversation and banter to a halt. Everyone turned to focus on him.

"I think now is the appropriate time to give my bride-to-be a wedding gift."

Cort handed Margaret a piece of paper. When she opened it, her eyes grew round with shock and surprise.

"What does it say, Mags?"

Margaret looked up at Cort and then over at her brother, replying with sheer joy in her voice. "It is the ownership papers on Chester, Cort's stallion."

"Correction, your stallion. I know you wanted to start a horse ranch, and now we can do that together. Although Chester may not compare with your Charlie, he is one of the best horses here in America."

Margaret pressed her lips together and fought back the

tears of happiness that were threatening to escape. All she had ever wanted was to be treated as an equal in a relationship, but she never thought it would actually happen. Cort's symbolic gesture showed he wanted her to be his partner in every aspect of their lives.

"No, he is a wonderful horse. In fact, when I saw him, I wanted to own him very much. Thank you, Cort. I know how much Chester means to you."

"Not as much as you."

Lady York asked, "Do you ride, Missus Learingam?"

"Yes, Lady Regina, as a matter of fact, I do. It is one of my favorite pastimes. My brother and I, as well as my sister-in-law, are all accomplished riders."

"Then I say we should all go riding sometime," added Lord Gregory.

"That would be smashing," interjected Randall.

"I say, it is very hard though to ride out here with the fear of being overtaken by Indians at any moment. I overheard about an attack on one of the homesteads nearby. It happened some months back. A woman and little girl were killed, and they still have not caught the Indians who burned the place to the ground," Lady Regina said.

Randall chimed in, saying, "It seems a lot of the townspeople have been talking about the Cheyenne attacks. I heard there have been several since the Sand Creek Massacre last year when soldiers killed Cheyenne and Arapahoe women and children at one of their encampments. Ever since, they have been retaliating by attacking settlers' homesteads."

"Yes, but that particular family could have been spared, had the husband been there to defend his homestead. Is that not absolutely appalling? You would think he would have stayed with them with the threat of Indians near," added Lord Gregory.

At the mention of the attack, Cort visibly stiffened. Noticing the tension in him, Margaret tilted her head and probed him with a look. Avoiding her gaze, Cort stood up, saying, "If you will excuse me, I just realized that I have something I need to take care of." Not waiting for a response, he walked out of the room.

Lord Gregory commented with a puzzled look, "I say, that sure was abrupt."

Not caring about anything but finding out what was wrong with Cort, Margaret made her excuses to the group. "I think I too will retire for the evening. Thank you for joining us, Lord and Lady York." Exiting, Margaret turned around and said to everyone, "Good evening."

Margaret picked up her skirt and rushed to catch up with her fiancé, who was already at the end of the hall. Once she reached him, she put her hand on his shoulder, stopping him. After a moment's pause, he turned around and she caught a glimpse of pain in his eyes before he hid it.

"You did not have to follow me."

"I wanted to."

"Yes, well, I am sorry to say, I think you will find I am bad company right now."

"I can see something upset you in there. What was it?"

For several seconds, he stared at her with a blank expression. Then he ran his hand through his hair in agitation. "The homestead that Lady York was talking about was mine."

Margaret rocked back on her heels, stunned from his revelation. "You mean it was your wife and daughter who were killed by Indians?"

"Yes."

Margaret stood rooted to the spot in astonishment. She did not know what to say. What could she say to that? He clearly was dealing with demons that had come from that event. What could she do to aid him? Perhaps just listening might help a little.

"Can you talk about it?"

He rolled his shoulders in frustration. "Lord Gregory was right. I was stupid, and I did not stay with my family like I should have. I knew about the Sand Creek Massacre and how the Indian tribes were furious. I knew better than anyone that settlers were not safe since my wife was half Sioux and they had warned her that the Cheyenne and Arapahoe had threatened to start attacking at the last inter-tribal meeting."

"But how were you to know that they would attack your place at that exact time?"

"Because there had been signs that a war party had

been around, but I thought I could leave for a few hours and nothing would happen. We were low on ammunition, and I worried we would not be able to defend ourselves if anything should happen, so I went into town to purchase some as well as look at a new mare for the ranch. I made a miscalculated decision and it cost me my family. I wish I had gotten home just a few minutes earlier. Even if I had not been able to stop them, at least I would have died protecting my family."

"I never want to hear you talk that way. If you had died that day with your family, we never would have met. I love you and need you. Besides, you had no idea what would happen when you left that day."

"Nothing you can say will change the fact that their deaths are my fault. My late wife's final words were 'I prayed you would come back and stop them,' but I failed her. I still struggle with why God did not bring me back in time to save them. I accept God allowed it to happen for a reason, but the pain and guilt still haunt me."

Margaret reached up and touched the side of his face. "You are a good man, Cortland Westcott. Do not ever doubt it. I would not be marrying you if it was not so."

He pulled her toward him and buried his face in her hair. After several seconds, he tilted his head so she could hear him whisper, "I thank God every day for you. He has blessed me with a gift that I do not deserve."

She wrapped her arms around his neck and ran her

fingers through his hair at the nape of his neck. "I love you."

He shifted so he could look into her eyes, then said, "And I, you."

"I am glad that you told me about this. It makes me understand you more." Then, as a thought struck her, she asked, "The Indians you helped us fight, where they the ones who attacked your place?"

"Yes, I had been tracking them for a few months, and I am quite certain the one who tried to scalp you was the one I saw crouched over Estella. I know now that I should not have sought revenge against the Cheyenne, but it was the only way I thought I could deal with my loss. I thought if I killed them, it might wipe away my guilt. But instead it has added to it and magnified what I already feel. Now I have their deaths on my conscience as well Estella's and Polly's."

"Was that your wife and daughter's names?"

He nodded.

"What were they like?"

"I did not have Polly for very long. She was only nine months when she passed away. She had the curliest brown hair I had ever seen, and she had the cutest smile that lit up her brown eyes when she giggled. My late wife, Estella, was the daughter of a California landowner. Different than you, she was Spanish and Indian, dark and earthy. I remember the few times I caught her cooking and she did not hear me come inside the cabin. She was so uninhibited, and she moved in such a graceful dance-like manner as she worked.

"Her father did not want her to marry me, but she went against him and did. That was why we moved out here to the Colorado Territory. We decided to start over where no one knew anything about us."

"She sounds wonderful," Margaret said softly. She did not know how to handle this. She felt as if now she had to compete with a ghost. His dead wife sounded majestic and perfect.

"She was"—he looked up at Margaret—"but so are you. And you are probably more suited for life out here than she had been. Estella hated living on the homestead. We had no servants and she was used to having many. She did not know how to take care of a place by herself, and she was not capable of adapting. Unlike you, she did not even know how to fire a rifle well. In addition, she hated living here and wanted more than I could give her."

"Just the same, it seems hard to compete with someone so extraordinary. My beauty pales in comparison to what you described."

Cort shook his head. "No, she was beautiful, but sadly, in many ways, her beauty was only skin deep. We had terrible fights. She was hotheaded and stubborn, like her father. And she was used to getting her way, since she was an only child and heir to one of the wealthiest landowners in the West. But I loved her."

He paused for a moment, then added, "She is gone now, and I have you. You are all I need and more in a wife. Do you not see that you are everything she was not and equally beautiful?"

She smiled. "Thank you for saying that."

"You do not believe me, do you?"

"I am trying to, really I am."

"You will see in time." Then after a moment's thought, he asked, "What about your late husbands? What were they like?"

Margaret stiffened at the mention of Henry and Michel. There was still so much pain from the losses.

"What? What did I say?"

"Nothing… it is only…. Can we go somewhere more discreet?"

Cort nodded and placed his hand under her elbow to guide her to a private sitting room next to the dining room they had just occupied.

Once inside, they sat on one of the sofas and Margaret continued. "Henry, my first husband, and I were both nobility in England. We had been betrothed since we were little. I did not think I loved him in the beginning when we were first married, but by the end, I was deeply in love with him."

"How did he die?"

Swallowing the lump in her throat, she replied, "He was killed by bandits."

Cort tipped his head to the side in question. Furrowing his brow, he asked, "How did that happen?"

Margaret pulled out of his embrace and turned her

back to him. She crossed her arms, trying to get a grip on the feelings spiraling inside her. "I was with child and wanted a doctor. While he was getting one, he was attacked. But it was not an accident. Someone deliberately set the bandits on my husband."

Cort pulled her around to face him. "I think you need to start at the beginning: names, places, events. I want to know you, Margaret. If we are to be married, there should be no secrets between us."

Trying to divert his attention, she retorted, "No secrets, you say? What about you?"

"What about me?"

"Where did you get your education, your obvious refined manners and speech? You surely did not pick them up out here. You may try to disguise who you are, Cortland Westcott, but I know that you are not simply some American cowboy."

"I am now, and that is all that matters."

"No, if I must tell you all the sordid details of my past, then you must tell me about your past too."

After several seconds, he said calmly, "I will tell you where I came from and how I ended up here, but only if you promise to do the same."

Margaret had not expected him to give in so easily. She thought about his offer. It was true, she was dying to find out who he was and about his life before he lived in America. But did she want to find out at the expense of telling him about her own past? Could she bear it? It was difficult enough to tell Michel and Randall. Could she handle the possibility that he might look at her differently after she told him? Would he even believe her?

She knew they should not have secrets between them, and it would only be a matter of time before it would have to come out. At least this way, it would be on her terms. It would be far worse if he found out by Witherton or Catherine showing up on their doorstep one day.

Before she knew it, she found herself saying, "I agree to your solution."

"Good." He took in a deep breath. "My real name is James Cortland Harring. I was born in England. I was the illegitimate son of a nobleman and a servant girl. I was the nobleman's first son, and even though I was not of titled blood, he took me in, educated me, and cared for me. A couple of years later, he had another son, who would inherit everything from our father, for his mother was my father's wife. She did not kick me out but allowed my father to keep me at the estate as long as it was made clear who the heir was at all times. But when our father died, my half brother decided he did not want me around. He was fearful that I would try to claim the title and lands for myself. Little did he know that I didn't want them. I never had. I would have much rather had a brother, but he made my life a living nightmare instead. So, finally, he got his wish. I left and entered the military. But his fear and hatred for me never let up until he finally framed me for desertion.

"I had been in the back alley of a bar in Paris when I

was attacked and beaten up. I was knocked unconscious and held somewhere—I do not know where exactly—until my ship had already left the harbor. They let me go, but I was considered a deserter, and if I had returned to England, I would have been hanged for treason. So I used the name Westcott, which I adopted from one of my fellow officers, and worked my way over here as a sailor on a commercial ship. It was on that ship that I found the Lord. It was an odd place to find someone who knew about Jesus, but the captain of the boat was a devoted Christian.

"At first, I was completely against hearing any of it. Being born into the circumstances that I had been, I was angry. I wondered, if God was real, why He would have allowed that, and all the other things, to happen to me. But Captain Luke was relentless, and he showed me the love of the Lord. He also helped me understand that God does not cause bad things to happen to people, but that Satan is the master behind the evil in the world. Captain Luke was the one who showed me that God is not capable of evil, only good, and that He loves everyone and only wants what is best for us. When I accepted the Lord on that cold November night, my life changed forever. The emptiness that had been in me went away, and I started reading my Bible and praying to the Lord all the time. The more I did, the better I felt and the more I started to change into a better person. I began wanting to put down roots and start a family, so I decided to make my way out to California as a hired hand on the wagon trail. I met Estella three years later at a ball after I had made quite a deal of money from buying and selling horses.

"It is funny, my brother probably thinks that he did me in and that he won, but the truth is, he set me free. I found the Lord because he made me leave everything I knew behind. I found two wonderful women to love and the chance to be a father, and that makes me the true winner, despite what he did to me."

"Have you seen or heard from your brother since you left Europe?"

"No, and I hope I never do."

"Do you ever want to go back?"

"Not really. I was no one there, just an illegitimate son of a nobleman. But here, I can make my own way and my own name. I do not need a title to achieve anything as long as I live in America." He looked at her and then asked probingly, "How did you end up here? Why did you leave your title behind?"

She cringed, thinking of the whole horrible affair. Noticing her reaction to his question, he stated, "You cannot back out. You agreed, remember."

"Yes, it is just hard." After pausing for a moment, she finally found the courage to continue after several seconds of silence. "I was born Margaret Elaine Wellesley, twin to Randall Thomas Wellesley, daughter to Lord Stewart Patrick Wellesley, Earl of Renwick. My mother, Lady Charlotte Elaine Sutton, Baroness of Ramlin, died giving birth to us. When we came over here, we took on our grandmother's maiden name, Learingam. I was betrothed to Henry William Wiltshire, the Viscount Rolantry, since I was a child."

Cort inhaled sharply and looked confused.

"What is it, Cort?"

He shook his head, replying, "Nothing. Keep going."

"But I fell in love with another man… the Duke of Witherton, Lord Richard Charles Crawley III. He courted me, sought after me, and even asked my father for my hand. But my father was a man of his word, and he had already promised me to Henry. So, even though I told my father I was not in love with Henry, he made me marry him anyway. Then I came to realize, over time, that I did love Henry, but had been hiding from it. I came to understand that I had merely been infatuated with Witherton and decided to make my marriage work. When I told this to Witherton, he was furious. You see, secretly, he had been trying to use me to get at Henry, but I was unaware of it at the time. He sent me a letter, telling me that he needed to meet with me or he would leak some scandalous things about Henry to everyone we knew. I know it seems stupid that I went alone, but I thought I was protecting my husband. When I got there, he attacked me. Henry arrived shortly after, invited by the duke as a trap, but he was able to stop him before he ruined me." Margaret paused and took a deep breath. It was so hard to say, even now, after all this time. She pushed back the tears, gripping her hands together in front of her.

"I am so sorry, Margaret, that *he* put you through that."

Margaret's eyes snapped up as she noticed the personalization in his tone when he addressed Witherton. Why did he do that? Wanting to finish as quickly as possible, she pushed Cort's reaction aside. "I thought we were finished with Witherton, but while I was pregnant with Henry's child, he had bandits attack Henry and kill him. I didn't know he was behind it until much later when he tracked me down in France and revealed the truth. You see, I had fled to France to escape Henry's sister, who believed the rumors and wanted to take my son from me to raise as the Rolantry heir without me in his life. I knew I had to leave England, and I wanted to go to France to look for my brother, Randall, who had gone missing years prior."

"That explains a lot of things, but why are you in America? And why are you using a different name without your titles?"

"We were very content in France. Randall met Jackie, or rather the Vicomtesse of Durante, and I was engaged to marry Lord Michel Robineau, the Marquis de Badour. But Witherton found me and tried to force me to marry him. I refused. I could never live with him or subject my son to his cruelties. Then he resorted to blackmailing me. He said he would tell Catherine where we were if I did not agree to his demands. I was able to get away from him and was determined to leave France, but Michel talked me into staying, believing he could protect us. Witherton tracked us down and attacked Michel, wounding him, but we thought he would recover. We were married but he died a few days later from an infection. I knew I had to leave Europe forever, and Randall and Jackie decided to come with me, as well as my two remaining loyal servants. We came to the Americas hoping to evade both Witherton and Henry's sister."

"I am so sorry all of that happened to you, Margaret. I will protect you with my dying breath. You do not have to be afraid any longer. I really believe God is going to use our relationship to mend your past."

She looked up at her husband-to-be and replied, "I think He is going to use me to do the same for you."

"He already has, Margaret. He knows exactly what He is doing. God gives you what you need, not always what you want. He knows I needed you and your son, and He brought you into my life at the exact time I was ready."

Margaret looked up into Cort's eyes and realized God had given her the man of her dreams in the most unexpected time and place. Cort was exactly what she needed, and God knew it.

CHAPTER 8

Margaret had never felt so beautiful as she looked at herself in the mirror. The local dressmaker had created an ivory satin gown with lace details at the neckline and on the edges of the sleeves and hem. It was simpler than her first wedding gown, and the one she had been fitted for in France, but she loved it. Because of her happiness, she felt the most settled she had in her life.

As she walked down the aisle in one of the hotel's private rooms, she saw Cort's loving grin and knew she was making the best decision of her life. He watched her intently as she approached him. She smiled as she took in his devastatingly handsome physique. He looked gorgeous in his perfectly tailored, cobalt blue suit.

Stopping at the front of room, she was greeted by Pastor Thompson. As Margaret looked around at her surrounding family and friends, she realized nothing could be more wonderful than that moment.

"Today, we come together to celebrate the long-awaited, blessed, and sacred union of Cortland Westcott and Margaret Learingam. We all saw the connection between the two of you when we were on the trail together and knew it was only a matter of time before Cort made you his wife." Pastor Thompson smiled at the two of them and gently patted Cort on the back. "It might have taken you longer than you expected to get her to consent, but you finally did it." Everyone in the room laughed at the unusual courtship of the couple.

"The two of you have chosen to join yourselves in the spiritual bond of holy matrimony. This is not something to enter into lightly. The commitment you make here today will bind you together forever, causing the two of you to be one for all eternity. The vows you will take today mean that no matter what may come into your lives, you will stand firm in your promises to each other and to God. Please face each other as you take your vows. Do you, Cort, promise to honor and love Margaret until death separates you?"

Cort squeezed Margaret's hands as he said, "I do."

"And do you, Margaret, promise to honor and love Cort until death separates you?"

"I do."

"Now that you have promised yourselves unto each other, it is time to bestow upon one another a symbol of the commitment you have chosen to make. Cort, as you place your ring upon Margaret's finger, please repeat after me." He paused, allowing Cort time to pull the ring from his pocket, and then continued, "With this ring, I promise my love and fidelity before the eyes of the Lord."

Margaret took her ring from Jackie and placed it on Cort's finger and repeated the same promise.

"With the blessing of God and before the eyes of man, I now pronounce you man and wife."

The newly married couple, turned to face the assembled guests and everyone began to clap and cheer for them as they stood side-by-side, hand-in-hand.

"Cort, you may now kiss your bride," Pastor Thompson proclaimed.

Turning to face each other, Margaret looked deep into Cort's memorizing hazel eyes. She knew marrying him was the best decision of her life and she could depend on him for anything.

As Cort bent down to kiss Margaret, for the first time since she could remember, she felt protected, safe, and secure. But most of all, she felt unconditional love.

After dinner with their guests, Margaret and Cort excitedly rushed into their wedding night.

Margaret grabbed Cort's arms with both hands, exclaiming, "We are married. I can hardly believe we did it."

"It feels amazing, does it not?"

"Yes, astounding."

As she entered into their suite at the inn, she stopped in her tracks as she looked around the room in awe.

The room was filled with fresh flowers in several arrangements around the room, amongst lit candles, casting a soft, romantic glow.

"Did you arrange all of this?"

"I wanted tonight to be special. After all you have been through, you deserve it."

"Just when I think you cannot treat me any better, you do something like this."

"I take it, you like it then?"

"Like it, I love it, Cort." As she turned to look at him, she added, "And I love you."

"I love you too, Margaret."

He pulled her into his arms and stared into her eyes for several moments. Then slowly, he leaned down and took her lips with his own. Margaret leaned into his embrace and sighed softly.

"I love you so much, Margaret." He brushed a few of her tendrils back that had fallen into her face as he smiled down at his wife with love and admiration.

Margaret beamed at the freshly built homestead in front of her before rushing forward, pulling Henry behind her. "It is beautiful, Cort."

Cort smiled with pride. "The house turned out better than I had imagined. I added a few features to the old place, like a storm cellar inside the house in case of Indian raids."

"Do we really have to worry about that?"

"Unfortunately, it is a part of frontier life. We always have to be prepared for it."

"I trust you, Cort. You know best."

"I am sorry we could not move in sooner, but they were still rebuilding it when we arrived in Boulder."

It had been a month since their wedding day, and they had spent the time living in the hotel in Boulder. It had been adequate but did not help them feel like they could plant roots.

"Mummy, this where we live?"

Margaret looked down at her son. "Yes, this is going to be our new home."

Cort came up behind them and put his arm around his wife, resting his other hand on the boy's shoulder. "Do you like the place, Henry?"

The boy answered Cort candidly. "It smaller than old house."

"Not surprising, but I think you will come to love it."

Henry did not reply, but instead opted to let go of his mother's hand and wander onto the porch. Cort turned his attention to his wife and smiled. "I think we will be very happy here."

"I think so too."

"Follow me, wife. I want to show you the part of our home you will be most interested in seeing."

"Where might that be, dear husband?"

"The stables, of course."

Margaret clasped her hands together in excitement. "I cannot wait."

As they made their way over to the stables, Cort explained that the structures surrounding the house had survived without catching fire when the Indians attacked.

When they arrived, Margaret heard several sets of hooves kicking in the dirt as well as horses neighing.

In the first stall was Chester, her wedding present from Cort, and in the next stall was Charlie. Both horses seemed to be content in their home. Margaret reached out and rubbed Chester's muzzle and the horse nickered in pleasure. "You are a good boy. Yes, you are, Chester. You are the best present ever."

Next to him, Margaret heard Charlie whine in protest. She moved over to stand in front of her jealous mare. "Now, Charlie, you need not be upset. You know you will always be my number one girl." She rubbed Charlie's crest as she hummed soothingly to her.

"You are so natural with them. I knew you were, but to watch you while you spend time like this makes me realize you are going to do great things with our horses."

Margaret looked over at her husband, who was staring at her with admiration in his eyes. She never thought she would find a man who would not only appreciate her dreams but share them. Cort wanted her to pursue her passions, and it touched her deeply.

"Thank you, Cort. It means more than you will ever know that you believe in me so much."

"You never have to worry about me trying to squash your independent spirit. I love that about you, and want you to always feel free to be yourself."

"Cort, You have given me everything I could ever want." She wrapped her arms around her husband's waist as he enfolded her in his embrace and rested his cheek on the top of her head.

"We are going to have a wonderful life together, Margaret."

Jackie came over a couple days later to join Margaret for afternoon tea. It was the one English tradition that Margaret refused to give up.

It turned out that they were neighbors since the land that Randall had inherited from their father was just a mile up the road. It was a nice place—a working ranch with a homestead.

Jackie was bursting with the need to tell Margaret the events that had taken place.

"Interestingly enough, when Randy went around inspecting our land, he found squatters on the banks of the river that runs along the edge of our property. When he asked them what they were doing there, they bashfully admitted they were prospecting for silver. Expecting him to kick them off our land, they started to pack their sparse belongings. But Randy surprised them, along with most of our other neighbors, by telling them not only could they stay, but they could keep mining on his land, so long as they gave him a quarter of their profits. They were so excited that they immediately went into their tents, pulled out what they'd already found, and on the spot gave him his quarter share. Of course, Randy declined it, telling them to reinvest that into equipment and that he only wanted his percentage from that point on."

With a laugh, Margaret said, "Rand may find himself making more from silver prospecting than from farming."

"Life here is not like it was back in France, that is certain, but then, I should never have expected it to be."

Margaret nodded. "I admit, it is hard to adjust when you have lived in Europe all your life. It is so different here. Life is rugged, and necessities shift from buying a new ball gown or hat to learning how to wash clothes by hand and how to shoot a gun."

"Yes, I admit, I am having difficulties with doing well with the whole gun issue. I have found that I am not an expert shot like you, Maggie."

Trying to be modest about her natural ability with a

gun, she shrugged. "I would not call me that exactly. More like a lucky shot, I would say."

It was Jackie's turn to laugh. "Hardly. I saw you when those Indians attacked us. You took several of them out before Cort even got there."

Margaret cringed, imagining what probably would have happened if Cort had not arrived when he did. "Yes, well, fortunately he did show up and we did not have to find out how good I really am."

"How are things going around here?"

"Good. Henry is adjusting well. He has been trying to help Cort around the place. I find it so adorable. He called him Papa the other day. It shocked me at first, but I am glad that he is accepting him as that."

"I was actually referring to the interaction between you and your husband. Are you adjusting to being married again?"

Margaret nodded. "It's easy with Cort. He treats me as an equal and wants my input regarding the horses and ranch. I never had that before."

After a pause, Jackie inquired, "How is Alfred settling into having Cort as the man of the house?"

"He enjoys having some time off from taking care of us. He says he's glad that he can help when he is needed, but he welcomes having time to read and paint."

"Paint?" Jackie asked in surprise. "I had no idea, Alfred could paint."

Margaret laughed. "Me either, but he's rather good at it."

"He deserves to have some happiness after all he has done for our family."

"Agreed." Margaret took a sip of her tea. "How are things between you and Rand?"

"Wonderful. That is why I came over today. I wanted to tell you some good news. I begged Randy to let me tell you, and he knew how much it meant to me, so he agreed."

"What is it?"

"I am pregnant," Jackie blurted out with a smile.

Margaret was surprised. She had not been expecting that kind of news. Frankly, the thought of Jackie being with child was odd. She could not even picture her with her belly protruding in any sort of way, let alone the way it would toward the end of a pregnancy. Even more of a strange thought was Randall as a father. But then, he was wonderful with Henry, so why would he not make a good one?

"You are not saying anything."

"Congratulations," Margaret said, with a touch of tension in her voice.

"Do you really mean it?"

"Of course, why would I not?" she said as she pasted on a strained smile.

"Well, it's just… you seemed so shocked."

"I was, but I think it is grand. You both will make wonderful parents. Really you will."

It was not that she was unhappy for them. It was the fact

that, all of a sudden, she was feeling an overwhelming desire to have Cort's child. She loved her son, but she wanted to give Cort a child of his own blood. Until the moment Jackie announced her pregnancy, she did not even realize the dormant desire existed.

"I am glad you think so. We are so thrilled about it, Maggie. I never thought I wanted to have children, but I love the thought that I am carrying Randy's child inside of me."

Margaret's eyes fell to Jackie's belly. She was suddenly filled with deep envy.

"It is a wonderful feeling, is it not?"

"Yes, nothing else compares to it. Not even that *other* stuff."

Margaret laughed, letting the comment break through the feelings racing in her.

CHAPTER 9

Over the past couple of months, Margaret, Cort, and Henry had been going to Pastor Thompson's church in Boulder, which was currently meeting in a framed schoolhouse while the new church was being built. Margaret continually found that not only did she enjoy Pastor Thompson's sermons, but she was also gaining more faith each week.

It was amazing having a faith-filled husband in her life. He encouraged her in the Lord daily and helped her to see that she could have a relationship with God like he had. They prayed when they woke up, before each meal, and at bedtime. Cort also read to the family every night out of their family Bible.

But even though she was growing closer to the Lord,

something ached inside her for change. She knew that a part of her was still damaged from her past and that she had never dealt with it. Rather than work on healing it, she had turned a blind eye to the damage and shoved it deep down inside.

She could see her own injured soul more clearly with each passing day and knew that something had to be done. She wanted to be whole again for her family, and part of that process was working at being the kind of wife and mother God would want her to be.

Getting the urge to make scones for her family, Margaret gathered the items from her pantry she would need. With bread and rolls for mealtime being a more practical use of their ingredients, she had refrained from making treats for the family in the past, but today, she wanted to splurge.

As she reached up and grabbed the flour off the top shelf, she thought about how it had taken a considerable amount of time for her to get used to the idea of having to take on all the chores her female servants used to do, but after each project she finished, she also felt a great deal of pride that she could do it herself—that she was making it as a frontier wife on her own.

When they arrived in Boulder, Sarah immediately received the attention of several available frontiersmen. Cort advised her on which ones would make a suitable husband, and after some prayerful consideration, Sarah married one of the local farmers. Though she only lives a few miles, away Margaret mostly saw her friend at church on Sundays and occasionally, in town at the general store.

This week had been especially difficult time since one of the colts died just after birth. Cort had been expecting a lot of this one since both her parents were of exceptional lines, and the loss stung deeply.

Margaret had been working with Charlie and getting her ready to accept Chester. She wanted it to go smoothly, and she knew that planning meant everything.

She smiled as she thought of Cort and how, just hours earlier, he had picked some wild flowers and brought them into her. It reminded her of a schoolboy bringing flowers to his first love. It was such a cute thing to do.

Henry scampered into the kitchen and pulled on his mother's skirt, asking, "When Papa coming in?"

Margaret had told Henry that he could no longer go out with Cort during work time—at least for the time being. Cort was breaking a few horses that he had bought from an Indian man the week before. She was afraid that Henry might get in the way and get hurt.

"He will be back in for lunch soon, Henry."

"Yea. I want play with him."

"He might be very tired, you know. Do not bother him too much."

"Okay, Mama. I miss him."

Margaret ruffled her son's hair as she laughed. "We just saw him a few hours back."

"It forever."

She shook her head. It was so funny how time passed for a child. Hours could seem like an eternity, and yet, when it came to bedtime, five more minutes could mean the world. "Go and play with your toys, Henry."

He nodded and hopped off to go play with his metal soldier toys by the windowsill.

Absentmindedly, Margaret wiped her face with her apron. The weather had really been getting to her. She was not used to the heat that they had here.

Trying to stop the dizziness, Margaret placed her hand on the edge of the stove and leaned against it. The dizzy spells had been coming more and more frequently the last week. She had not told anyone about them because she thought they would pass, as she just needed to adjust to the new weather.

She shook her head as she began to see spots. This was not good. She needed to go lie down just for a moment, until it went away.

Margaret turned around slowly and started to head for the hallway, but before she made it, she lost control and everything began to spin. Before she knew it, she was falling, and then she felt herself hit the ground hard. As darkness closed in, she could hear Henry in the background, calling to her and shaking her shoulder.

She wanted to respond and tell him everything would be all right, but nothing would come out. Instead, she welcomed the blackness that claimed her and took the pain away.

Margaret woke to find herself lying in their bed. She was confused. Had she not been in the kitchen baking?

"The scones. They are going to burn."

"No, sweetheart, they're fine. That was a day ago."

When Margaret looked at her husband, she noticed the deep pockets of black under his eyes. Whatever happened to her must have taken a bad toll on him. "A day ago? Why can I not remember anything since then?"

"You have been unconscious ever since it happened, and the doctor said it was best if we let you rest. He said that you haven't been drinking enough water and the heat had gotten to you."

"Oh, is that all? I thought it might have been something worse."

"Well, there is more."

"Pardon?" She braced herself for the bad news.

"The doctor believes you to be with child, Margaret. I told him you had been fatigued lately along with feeling sick in the mornings and periodic dizzy spells, all of which are common symptoms of the condition."

Margaret was bewildered. Why did she not know? It was her body, and yet, she had had no idea that she was with child. She had never experienced any of those things while she carried Henry.

"Is he sure?"

"He needs to ask you a few questions to confirm it, but

he believes he is correct." Cort frowned. "Are you not happy?"

"Quite, but I just do not understand why I did not know."

"I asked him the same thing, and he said that the change in weather might have kept you from noticing. He said it was quite common and happens when you are new to the area."

"I am glad to hear that, then." Margaret raised her eyes from where they had been staring in her lap to meet his. "How do you feel about it?"

When he looked at her for several seconds without showing any emotion, Margaret tensed with apprehension. What if he was not happy about the baby? What if it was too soon or he did not want to have any more children after losing his infant daughter, Polly?

Then, as if he sensed her fears, he took her hands in his and smiled. "I am happier than I can ever remember. This is the best news any man can be given. I always wanted a big family."

"I am glad to hear you say that, Cort." She looked around their room and glanced toward the door. "Is Jackie here?"

"Yes, both she and Randall have been waiting outside. They are anxious to see that you are all right."

"Have you told them?"

"No, I wanted to wait until you had awakened so that we could tell them together."

"Can you bring them in?"

"Yes, I will go get them."

Cort stepped outside the room, closing the door behind him. A few moments later, he ushered them inside.

Margaret was sitting up in bed with her hands folded in her lap. She had tried to comb her hair with her fingers to tame the mass of curls, but resorted to scooping them up and clipping them with a barrette that had been on the nightstand.

"How are you feeling, Mags?"

"Perfectly all right, Rand."

"Do you hurt anywhere or feel feverish?"

"No, truly, I feel wonderful."

Randall smiled, which helped to lighten the bags that were under his eyes. "Good to hear. We have not been able to sleep a wink since we heard. Jackie especially."

"Oh, I am sorry to have worried you both—especially in your condition, Jackie."

"Yes, but I am doing well, chéri. It is you who we should be worrying about. What exactly happened?"

"Well, that is why Cort and I wanted you to come in now. We needed to tell you something."

Jackie looked from Margaret to Cort and back to her sister-in-law; it appeared she suspected the worse.

"What is it, Maggie? It is not fatal, is it?"

Margaret laughed lightly, realizing that their serious looks must have frightened her. "No, not quite, Jackie, but what I have is not going away any time soon. You see, I am also with child."

Jackie and Randall both looked surprised. "Oh, but you frightened us so. This is good news, no?"

Margaret turned to Cort, who was standing at the end of the bed, and reached out her hand to her husband. "Yes, very."

"Then why the long faces?" asked Randall in an accusing voice.

Cort went to his wife's side, took her hand in his, and knelt beside her. "We are still taking all this in ourselves."

"Well, let me be the first to congratulate you. It seems we are both going to be fathers soon."

Cort smiled, "Yes, although I already am one."

It took Randall a moment to realize that he was referring to Henry. "Oh yes, it has been jolly good of you to take Henry as your own. But now you will have another little one to bring you even more joy."

"Yes, it will be good to hold a baby again."

Randall raised an eyebrow quizzically. Neither Margaret nor Cort had told either of them about his past. But before Randall could question him, the door was thrown open and Henry rushed into the room, jumping on top of his mother.

"Mama, Mama, you're better."

Cort reached for him. "Henry, you should not jump on your mother like that. She has been very sick and needs to be treated gently."

She wrapped her arm around her son protectively. "It is all right, Cort. Let him stay. It feels good to hold him."

"Henry, we have some good news to tell you."

"What is it, Mama?"

"It seems that you are going to have a new baby brother or sister."

"Really? Where is he?"

She laughed and then added, "Not this moment, darling, but in a few months from now. And it might be a girl just as easily as a boy."

"I hope it's a boy so I can play with him."

"You can play with a girl too, you know."

He frowned. "I don't like girls."

"Oh, is that so? Well, I am a girl."

"No, you're not. You're my mama."

Randall ruffled his nephew's hair, then chimed in, "Sisters are not so bad." He winked at Margaret. "After all, they can be fun every once in a while."

"Really, Uncle Randy?" In the beginning, Henry struggled with calling him Randall and had picked up the habit of calling him Randy from Jackie.

"Yes, your mother is a wonderful gal. She is almost like one of the chaps."

Margaret slapped him playfully. "Oh posh. Do not tell him such things. He will take you seriously."

"No I won't. Uncle Randy is never serious."

They all laughed at that, knowing how close to the truth it was.

Henry jumped off his mother and ran from the room singing, "We're going to get a baby. We're going to get a baby."

Margaret smiled as she listened to him sing of the good news. It seemed that her prayers had been answered.

"I'm so glad that you are here to share in our happiness."

Randall smiled at his sister and then his own wife. "We are glad that you wanted us to share in your celebration. Which brings us to a question we have for the both of you. We planned to ask you at the next family dinner, but now is as good a time as any."

"What is it, Rand?"

"We would be honored if the both of you would agree to be our baby's godparents."

Margaret looked at Cort expectantly, who nodded. "Yes, it seems we are twice blessed today. Not only are we going to be parents again, but we are going to be godparents as well."

"So, how did the two of you decide that you wanted to follow this tradition?" Cort asked.

Randall looked at his wife, who was in turn smiling at everyone. "A few days ago, I asked Jackie how she felt about the religious tradition of godparents, and she told me she had never really thought about it. But I made it clear that, if anything should ever happen to us, I wanted our child to be raised by parents who would take care of them the way we would."

"Yes, I see your point, Randall. And that gives me an idea. How would you feel about returning the favor and being our children's godparents?"

"I would consider it an honor. What do you say, Jackie?"

"I would love to be your children's godmother."

"Good, it's settled. We know now that our families will be taken care of no matter what," Cort said with a smile.

CHAPTER 10

A man she could not make out knocked her to the ground. Cort was a few feet from her and she was trying to reach out to him, but before she could, the other man stepped in between them.

Hearing the voice of the other man, she tried to make out what he was saying, but it was muffled.

Fear overwhelmed her as she tried to get up to help Cort. She knew the man between them wanted to kill him; she could hear the hate in the tone of his voice.

When she heard a gunshot, Margaret screamed, and then darkness enveloped her.

A hand landed on her shoulder, and she heard Cort whisper, "It is all right, Margaret. You are safe. I am right here, sweetheart." She opened her eyes but still felt disoriented. She jerked away from his touch. Apparently, she had been crying and mumbling in her sleep.

"What is wrong, Margaret? What happened?"

Her eyes darted around the room, and when she finally focused her eyes on Cort, she sighed from heavy relief.

"Cort, you're all right. I was so frightened. I thought you were in trouble, and I was so scared. There was gunfire and something so sinister. I didn't know what to do."

He pulled her into his arms. "I'm here, and I'm never going to let anything happen to you. I will protect you with my life."

She knew she should feel relief, but it was exactly what Margaret was afraid of him having to do. Steadily, for two weeks, she had the same nightmare. Each time, it brought more dread, because deep down, she knew the dream was going to come true. She did not know when or how, but it was only a matter of time. She knew something awful was on the horizon.

The heat was now taking its toll even worse as Margaret struggled to continue to do her normal chores. She hadn't felt this bad since the first few weeks of the pregnancy. She had told Cort about the dizzy spells that had been coming on regularly the last week. He had made sure to have plenty of water brought up from the well so she would not get dehydrated again. She was told by the doctor that, as long as she drank plenty of water and took a rest when the symptoms started, the dizzy spells would pass.

The time for the baby's birth was quickly approaching. She was already moving into her sixth month. She smiled as she thought about their future, temporarily forgetting about the sickness she was feeling.

She was finally reaching the point where she could accept that things were going to continue to get better. Every day, she had less and less fear that either Witherton or Catherine would find them. And with that peace, she was finally able to focus on the future of her family.

But even though she felt her life could not be any more perfect, something still felt like it was missing. There was still a pain deep inside her, and she didn't know how to mend it. What would it take for her to feel whole again?

Margaret had just started to clean again when another wave of dizziness hit her. She leaned against the nearby wall and waited for it to pass. But this time, it did not.

Rest… she just needed to rest. If she lay down, it would pass quicker.

Margaret made her way toward her bedroom, stopping to check on Henry. She bit her lip to block out the sickness as she leaned against the doorframe of his room. Content he was sleeping peacefully, she continued to her own room. Once inside, Margaret sat on the edge of her bed and unbuttoned the top couple of buttons of her dress. It was so hot.

Wiping her forehead with the back of her hand, Margaret laid back onto the bed, letting out a quiet sigh as her body relaxed. The tension started to drain away.

"See, all I needed was a few minutes to rest," she said to herself.

Hearing a noise outside, she jumped up with a start. Then, realizing it was Cort coming back from town, she quickly buttoned up her dress and left the bedroom.

She glanced in the room to see if the noise had woken Henry. As she suspected, he was sitting up and quickly pulling on his shoes.

"Is that Father? Is he home?"

Margaret nodded and smiled. "I believe so."

Henry jumped up and ran across the room. But as he tried to run past her through the door, she grabbed his arm. "Oh no, you do not. Wait for me."

Henry bunched his eyebrows together in frustration as he looked up at her. "Oh, Mama."

She took his hand and pulled him behind her, saying, "Remember what I taught you. Manners matter when no one else is around just as much as when many are present. Running around like a wild Indian does not reflect well on either of us."

Henry hung his head and replied in a whisper, "Yes, Mama."

Hearing the hint of shame in his voice, Margaret stopped walking and turned to face her son. She lifted his face so that his eyes met her own.

"Henry, I am very proud of you. You are the best son anyone could ask for. I only want the best for you, and that is why I tend to be strict with you. My father tried to be the same with me, and at the time, I did not see it, but it was for my own good. I love you. You know that, do you not?"

"I do, Mother."

"Good, and do not forget it." She winked at him. "Let us go meet your father."

As they entered the living area, Alfred was in the kitchen with the storm cellar open. He had a large jug in his arms. "I am just putting this inside with the rest of the provisions. Having some water stored seems practical."

"I just heard a noise outside. I think Cort is home."

"I will finish this up, and then go help him unload the supplies."

"Thank you, Alfred."

As she approached the door, Margaret had an odd feeling that something was not quite right. It was as if God was telling her to be careful. Things were not as they appeared. She put Henry behind her, pausing, then said in a whisper to him, "Go into the kitchen, Henry, and wait with Alfred there."

"I want see Papa."

"I said, *go* into the kitchen."

She felt him turn around and head toward the kitchen, muttering something about it not being fair. Once she knew he was safely out of view, she grabbed the handgun by the door, which was loaded, and put it in the pocket of her apron. Then she grabbed the rifle, which was also loaded, and took a deep breath.

Throwing open the door, she raised the gun in anticipation. To her surprise, she saw no one. Where was Cort? She did not hear anything. In fact, it was eerily quiet, like everything was standing still and nature was holding its breath.

Margaret started to lower her gun and step back into the house when she saw movement out of the corner of her eye.

She swiveled to the side, keeping the gun supported against her shoulder.

She gasped in shock and fear. There was a young Indian near the corrals, glaring back at her with a knife in his hand. Margaret forced herself to keep her arms steady. She had to maintain control of the gun or it was all over.

"You need to leave now."

A sadistic grin spread across his lips as he shook his head. "No, you drop gun."

She pressed her lips together, trying not to show her fear. "If you leave now, we will forget this happened. You can leave with your life."

"You woman. You not hit me."

"You are a fool if you believe that. I warn you, I'm a crack shot. I can sure enough hit you," she yelled at the man. She kept the gun raised and waited for the Indian's next move. When nothing happened, Margaret asked angrily, "What do you want?"

"You."

Margaret licked her lips as fear seized her insides. She had heard the rumors of what Indians did to their captives. There was no way she was going with him willingly.

"What do you mean, me?"

"You drop gun, come here."

"This is your last chance. I am warning you, leave my land now!"

She saw him start to move towards her, quickly closing the distance. Reflexively, she pulled the trigger.

She heard the loud crack of the rifle and felt the recoil push against her body. It did not faze her as she prepared to fire again, planting her feet squarely and firmly on the porch. She looked to see if she had indeed hit her target.

Her eyes met the Cheyenne warrior's, and she recognized the shocked look in his eyes as blood started to pour out of the wound in his right shoulder.

Unfortunately, he was still holding the knife. She had hoped the impact of the bullet would have made him drop it. No such luck. Margaret watched in horror as he stalked toward her, his hand gripping the knife with anticipation.

She raised the rifle but not in time to stop him. He knocked it out of her hands and grabbed her.

He glared at her, then stated with disgust, "You shoot me."

"And I would do it again," she said in defiance.

He slapped her in the face. "You not speak me that way."

Margaret tried to block out the throbbing flooding her face. She had never been hit before, and it hurt much more than she would have thought. Pushing the pain away, she concentrated on getting the handgun out of her pocket. She pulled the weapon free before the Indian even realized what it was. "I warned you," she said as she fired.

She stepped back as he fell forward and hit the porch. He rolled onto his side and let out a savage scream.

It was only then that she realized he was probably not alone.

Just as she suspected, two more Indians came from around the sides of the house. Holding the handgun in front of her, Margaret quickly stepped back into the house, shutting the door behind her and bolting it.

She grabbed the last handgun on the rack by the door and ran toward the kitchen. Once inside, she glanced around, and panic flooded her when she did not see him anywhere.

"Henry?" she whispered in a frightened voice.

After a few seconds, she heard a murmur from the cellar. She looked down into it and found him crouched at the bottom of the stairs next to Alfred.

She recognized the terror in her son's eyes as he asked, "What happening, Mama?"

"Henry, I want you to stay in the cellar with Alfred. I want you to be as quiet as possible. Do not open it or come out, no matter what. *No matter what*, you stay in there until your father comes to get both of you. Do you understand me?"

His eyes were round with fright as he nodded.

"What are you planning to do, my lady?" Alfred asked with worry.

"They have seen me, and they will not give up until they find me. The only chance the both of you have is if you hide in here and I keep their attention somewhere else."

Margaret heard the Indians trying to bust in the door. It was barred shut but would only keep them out for a few more minutes at best.

She handed Alfred the pistol. "Shoot only if you have to. The noise will draw them."

"I'm scared," Henry whimpered.

"I know, darling, but it's going to be all right."

She hugged him and whispered in his ear, "I love you, son. Never forget that."

"Come in, Mama."

"I cannot, Henry. I have to stay out here. Be strong for me, darling."

"I will."

She closed the door, replaced the rug and table, and left the kitchen, not wanting to attract attention to that room if she could avoid it.

She went to the bedroom and barricaded the door. All she could do was wait them out and pray to God that He would bring help.

CHAPTER 11

Cort knew something was wrong the moment he got back home. He narrowed his eyes and scanned the area as he made his way toward the house with fear and dread, terrified of what he would find.

As he made his way onto the porch, he stepped over the dead body of an Indian, he glanced down at him and frowned. The Indian seemed familiar. Why was that?

Not having time to think about it, he stepped into the house and made his way through each room.

He tried to block out the memories that were flooding his mind. It was not the same. The house was not burning, which meant they did not just attack for a whim. There was a reason behind it.

It looked as though Margaret had made her stand in the

bedroom. She seemed to have held them off for a while, but they had managed to get in through one of the windows.

There was no sign of anyone. He didn't even see any evidence that Alfred had been with them. Did they take them? Sometimes they took white women and children as slaves.

Then Cort remembered the cellar he had put in. Yes, that was it.

He ran to the kitchen, threw the table out of the way, and moved the rug.

"Anyone in there?"

"Papa?"

Cort sighed with relief and flung open the cellar door.

"Yes, it's me, son."

Henry looked up timidly from the bottom of the steps. Relief flooded the boy's face. Alfred was sitting next to him and the concerned look didn't leave his face.

Henry rushed up the stairs, falling into his father's arms. "I glad you here."

"Are you all right?"

"Yes… where Mama?"

"Isn't she with you?"

"No." The boy's bottom lip started to quiver. "She okay?"

Cort forced a smile for Henry's sake. "I'm sure she is, champ. We just have to find her."

"Where Mama?"

"I do not know, but I'll get her back," he said with steely determination. "Don't you worry."

He stood up and looked at his son. "Pack a few things. You're going to be spending a few days at your Aunt Jackie and Uncle Randall's house."

Henry headed for his room without complaint.

"Alfred, I want you to go with Henry."

"But I would rather aid you in finding Mistress Westcott."

Shaking his head, Cort stated, "I want you to continue to keep Henry safe. Can you do that for me?"

Alfred nodded as followed after Henry.

Cort continued to look around. It felt like he was missing something, almost like there was a clue as to what happened that he was not seeing.

He went back out onto the porch and looked down at the Indian. They usually took their dead if they could. They had plenty of time to take him with them. That meant they must have left him for a reason.

Crouching down, he turned the Indian's face from side to side. He seemed so familiar. Then he realized why. He was one of the Cheyenne who had attacked his place the last time, and he was one of the Indians who attacked Margaret's party on the trail.

So, there was a connection. They must have waited for him to leave to attack. He was a fool for leaving them. There had been no warning signs of nearby Indians, but he should have been more careful. He left a defenseless young woman, and old man, and a little boy to fend for themselves. Now Margaret was missing, and he was to blame again.

Cort stood and started to walk back into the house, but stopped when he saw something pinned to the doorframe. He looked closer and sucked in a deep breath. It was Margaret's wedding ring attached to a bloody piece of buckskin. So, this was a retaliation of some sort, possibly a blood debt. They took her because they were expecting him to come after her. But he knew they had no intentions of letting either of them live.

And the baby. *My God, Margaret is pregnant. This might cause her to lose the baby.*

He had to stop thinking about all that and focus on getting her back. If she was…. He could not think of that. He had to keep believing she was alive or he was not going to make it through this. He loved her so much, he did not know what he would do if they harmed her. Nothing else mattered except finding her.

He grabbed the ring and buckskin, wrapped them up together, and put them in his pocket. It was time to go get his wife.

Randall opened the door and found Cort on the other side.

"What's all the pounding about?"

"Our homestead was attacked by Indians. Margaret has been taken captive. I came to ask you, as Henry's godparents, to watch over him while I go after Margaret. I brought Alfred along too. It's not safe at our place."

Jackie came up behind her husband. "Of course, we will take care of both of them."

Cort gestured to Henry to walk inside. "Thank you for letting them to stay here," Cort said, as he placed Henry's sack of belongings inside the front entry of their house.

Jackie nodded as she extended her hand to her nephew. "Are you hungry, Henry? I just made some soup for supper."

The boy took Jackie's hand and whispered, "Yes, Aunt Jackie, it sounds good."

After they left the room, Randall turned to face Cort. "Let me gather a few things before we head out."

"Your baby is due in a few weeks, which is exactly why you are not coming with me. You need to be here for your wife," Cort argued.

"On the contrary, Margaret saved my life back in France, and now it's time for me to return the favor. I am coming whether you like it or not, so just accept it."

Cort forced a grim smile. "All right. I probably need all the help I can get."

They had been following their tracks for over five days now. Cort had a renewed respect for Margaret's brother. He had managed to keep up and not complain about anything. Randall was a lot like his sister. He saw the same determination in Randall to find Margaret that was such an intricate part of Margaret's character.

Margaret.... If they hurt her, he knew it just might drive him over the edge. Right now, all that was holding him together were two things. He realized that she was still alive and counting on him to save her, and most importantly, God was on his side. He had peace that only God could give him. He was sustaining Cort and guiding him.

Cort knew God had brought them together and God would restore their family. Cort could see that there was still pain from Margaret's past that she had not given to the Lord. Even though her love for God was apparent, she still wanted control of her life. Because her whole life had always been decided for her by others, she was scared to give up authority to anyone, even her Creator. God was not done with Margaret, and He had promised Cort that he was going to make her whole again. God would not let her die until that promise was fulfilled. He knew this, and it was the ultimate reason that kept him going. Wherever she was, he knew she was alive.

"What are you thinking about? You have an odd look on your face."

Noticing that there had been an abrupt change in direction, Cort was filled with worry. From the marks in the dirt, it looked like there had been a scuffle between a few of the Indians over something. "It seems that our *friends* had an argument and parted ways. Two of them went this way and the other three went in the other direction, taking Margaret with them."

"You can tell all that from those markings in the ground?"

Cort nodded but did not enlighten him with the information that he had been a scout and guide during his time in the military. He did not want to have to explain everything right now.

"It seems you have many hidden talents."

Cort looked at Randall and raised an eyebrow in amusement, then grinned. "Yes, well, I like to keep people guessing."

"You manage quite nicely, I say."

"Thank you. I'll take that as a compliment."

"You would."

Cort shrugged. "We need to keep going."

Randall pulled back on his reins and his horse started trotting as he turned his head and shouted, "Are you coming?"

Without saying a word, Cort nudged his horse forward with his spurs and followed his friend.

CHAPTER 12

When the Indians first took her hostage, Margaret had been terrified. They looked at her as if she were not even there, just a pawn they planned to use.

She had assumed they would at least take into account her obvious state of being with child, but that also had no effect on them. Every minute, she feared she would lose the baby.

She was exhausted from their never-ending travel. They never stopped, just kept pushing forward. But to where? She had no idea where they were taking her.

They had bound her hands with rope and tied her to the saddle of one of the horses—as if she truly were an animal that they had trapped.

In the beginning, Margaret had managed to keep up

due to the protection from her boots. As the conditions of the path worsened, her feet began to crack and bleed, causing every single step to be excruciating. She forced herself not to dwell on it, but prayed internally for God's protection and mercy until Cort found her.

"So, explain to me, Cort, how did you know what those markings in the path meant back there?"

Cort pushed the smoldering pieces of wood around in the fire while he sat quietly pondering how to answer.

"I was in the Royal Army several years ago. I was trained to be a tracker and guide."

"Really? How long were you in Her Majesty's Army?"

"Five years."

"And you tracked for that whole time?"

"No, I advanced up the ranks and was a lieutenant toward the end."

"It sounds like you were planning on making it a career. Any particular reason why you left?"

"You could say that."

"Do you mind enlightening me?"

"I was framed for desertion."

"Come again?"

"Someone had it out for me and set me up to look like a deserter. When we were on shore for a short leave, this person had a few thugs waiting outside a bar for me. They beat me to a bloody pulp and hid me away in some remote place. By the time I got out of there, my ship had set sail without me. When I made it back to England, they were looking for me to throw me into prison. I managed to get out of town before they could locate me."

"But I am sure you had friends higher up in the chain of command. Why did you not have one of them fix things?"

"The man who framed me was quite powerful. Escaping to America was my only option."

"This enemy of yours sounds like a nasty brute. What did you do to earn his wrath?"

"Guilt by relation. I am his half brother."

"What does that have to do with anything?"

"He viewed me as a threat to his 'kingdom' that he was going to inherit. But the ridiculous part of it all was that, even if I had wanted to try to claim it, I could not have."

"Why is that?"

"You see, Randall, I am illegitimate. You know English law as well as anyone. If you are not legitimate, you cannot inherit anything. Besides, I never wanted any of it anyway. I never did understand why he was so determined to get rid of me."

"So, you left just like that? It could not have been that easy leaving the country."

"It was not. I was lucky and had the help from a few loyal friends."

"You seem to be careful in what you are telling me. Why?"

Cort sighed in exasperation. He might as well tell him everything or he was just going to keep hounding him. It was smarter if he just told him and made him swear not to tell Margaret.

"Because there is more to this story and I have not told any of it to Margaret."

"Why have you not told her?"

"It is safer if she does not know."

"Well, what is it?"

"My half brother is the Duke of Witherton."

Randall inhaled sharply and then stared at Cort for several seconds. "What are the odds of that?"

"Incredibly slight."

"What are you implying?"

"I think that God is at work in this somehow. I am not sure why, but I have a feeling that it will become clear once things have played out."

"You do know that the duke is the reason we fled here to the Americas."

"Yes, Margaret told me that."

"Do you also know what he did to her first husband, and her fiancé, Michel?"

"Yes, I know that too."

"He has been tracking us. It is only a matter of time until he finds her and my nephew again."

"I realize that as well."

"What do you plan to do when he finds her?"

"I plan to rid all our lives of him permanently."

Randall nodded, accepting Cort at his word. "There has been something else that has been bothering me ever since I found out about the child you are expecting."

"What is that?"

"You said, 'It will be good to hold a baby again.' What did you mean by that?"

Cort grit his teeth together, fighting back the dark feelings that flooded him. What was going on now was so close to what he had gone through with Estella's and Pollina's deaths that it brought back all the old, horrible feelings. Worse, there was a sense of urgency to act fast because he was racing against time in order to get to Margaret before they harmed her.

He did not want to talk about this, and it frustrated him that Randall was far more observant than he had given him credit for in the beginning.

"When I fled here, I started completely over. For a few years, I was alone until I met Estella. We got married and had a daughter. I was speaking of holding her."

"What happened to them?"

"I left them alone and Indians attacked the homestead. They killed them both."

"My God, Cort, I am sorry."

"Yes, well, I wish it had ended there. But I went after them and that's when I came across your party. We wounded and killed several of them, but as you know, some escaped. It was the remnants of that war party who attacked our place and took Margaret captive."

"I see."

"I doubt it. You see, they came after me and took Margaret as leverage. She is bait, and once they have me, they will kill us both. I believe it is a blood vengeance for one of the Cheyenne I killed."

"This seems to be just one giant bloody mess, does it not?"

"That it does, Randall. That it does."

Margaret's group arrived in the Indian camp at dusk. The people who greeted them were not friendly to the stranger; some looked at her skeptically while others scowled at her. The children ran after them and yelled at her.

Margaret closed her eyes as they paraded her down the middle of the camp. She did not want to see the mocking faces glaring at her. Instead, she pinched her eyes tightly shut and prayed to God.

Oh Lord, please help me now. I do not have the strength to carry on anymore. I cannot take anything else these people may do to me. Protect me in this most vulnerable hour.

When she opened her eyes, she found herself standing in front of an older Indian who she assumed was the chief of the tribe due to the headdress he was wearing and the respect he garnered from all the other members. He was staring at her, not with the contempt the others had shone, but rather with what seemed to be a mixture of curiosity and something else—something that shot chills up Margaret's back.

He turned his head to the left and said something to the woman next to him. After a moment, the woman, who seemed to be the chief's servant, turned and entered the tent behind them.

The chief then said something in their native tongue and motioned for the leader of the war party to come forward. She held her breath, knowing that right then, the two men were deciding what was to be done with her.

At first, the conversation seemed to be going smoothly, but then there was some sort of disagreement between the two men. The leader of the war party was gesturing toward her, and the chieftain was shaking his head as he folded his arms across his chest in what looked to be a resolved decision.

The chief's servant came out of the tent, carrying what appeared to be an Indian girl's dress and moccasins. The woman returned to her spot next to the chieftain, holding the articles of clothing in her arms.

The chief grunted and motioned toward Margaret. Two of the Cheyenne warriors who had helped capture her forced her forward and onto her knees in front of the old Indian and then stepped back.

Without any warning, he reached out and grabbed her roughly by the arms. Margaret squelched her desire to scream in fear. She forced herself to stay perfectly still and tried not to shake as best she could. The two times she had been kidnapped had taught her to show as little weakness as possible.

Angered by her lack of visible fear, he glared at her for several seconds.

Margaret tried not to flinch with his face only inches away from her own. She wondered what he was thinking. What was he planning on doing with her? Would they kill her immediately or keep her as a trophy?

Slowly, a sneer crossed the chief's face as he grunted a second time before letting go of her and taking the clothes from his servant. When he threw them down on the ground in front of her, she mechanically picked them up. He pointed to the clothes in her hands and said, "You put on now."

She blinked and started to step around him to go into the tent, but he put out his arm, saying, "No, put on here."

Margaret swallowed the lump in her throat. Somehow, when she thought the degradation could get no worse, these people managed to find a way. The thought of all these people seeing her in her undergarments made her seethe with fury. This latest antic might be her undoing. She did not know if she could keep it together, but she reminded herself that she needed to do what they said until Cort could find her.

She dropped the Indian clothes in front of her and took in a deep breath as her hands fluttered to the top buttons of her light blue and white gingham blouse. With shaky fingers, she managed to undo the buttons of her blouse. She shrugged it off and picked up the squaw dress. She stood up and slipped on the dress over her shift, then pulled off her skirt from underneath. When she was done, she lifted her chin in quiet defiance.

The chief shouted something in a mocking tone and everyone around her started to laugh. Margaret clenched her teeth and narrowed her eyes in anger. She hated being laughed at more than anything. She balled her hands into fists, fighting back the urge to do something reckless.

For several moments, they laughed, pointed at her, and made cruel comments that were clearly about her. She continued to keep her eyes averted and her face and body void from showing any emotions.

The chief watched her closely for several seconds before yelling something to the crowd around them. Abruptly, everyone stopped and turned their attention to him. He raised his hands and made a motion, causing the people to disperse until it was just the two of them left alone.

"You come with me, Heart Full of Fire."

Margaret frowned as she followed the chief into his tent. "Why did you call me that?"

"I see fire in heart. You try to hide, but I see. I know it there. You can fool others, not me."

"I was not trying to fool anyone. I was doing what I had to in order to survive."

"You wish to survive?"

"Yes, more than anything."

"What so important?"

"My children."

"Children?"

"Yes, I have a son back home and a child"—she rested her hand on her stomach—"on the way."

The chief's eyebrows burrowed together as he grunted, then said, "What of husband?"

"Yes, I wish to survive for him as well."

"And he come for you?"

"Yes, he will. As the very air I breathe, I know he is coming for me."

"Good."

A look of surprise crossed Margaret's face as she asked, "Why is that good?"

"That what we want."

"I do not understand."

"Death for death."

CHAPTER 13

Even as an expert tracker, Cort was having a difficult time following the Indians who took Margaret.

"Do you think we are getting closer?"

"I hope so. It has been two days since we lost their trail."

"It was a lot of bad luck, that sandstorm."

"Yes, it has managed to make things much harder."

"Do you think…? I mean, would they hurt her?"

"I pray to God they will not, but I do not know. They are not known for being kind to their captives."

"Yes, well, if any woman could hold their own with a bunch of savages, it would be Mags."

"Yes, I am sure if they did try anything, she would make it pretty difficult for them."

"Let us hope it never comes to that."

Margaret pushed her wet hair off her face and grabbed the edge of the blanket to wipe the sweat from her brow. Having another sleepless night, she took deep breaths, trying to calm herself before getting up.

She could not let her captors see the fear in her. They would use it against her. She had managed to survive two weeks without being abused; she could make it until Cort got there if she was cautious.

She placed her hand on her stomach as her baby kicked softly against her. It comforted her to feel the little life still thriving within her. She would do whatever it took to keep her baby safe.

Once she had herself under control, she quickly stood up and felt the cold breeze against her cheek.

Even though she hated being at the Indian camp and despised being their captive, she also acknowledged their lives were simpler, and therefore easier in some ways. They did only what they needed to live. They did not kill themselves to gain more than what they needed. But although she could respect how little they cared for material possessions, there were also negative things about their way of life. They treated women even worse than her society did. Women were little more than dogs to them. They used them and treated them as slaves.

Anxiously, she waited each day, hoping that Cort was going to arrive to free her and take her home. Yet part of her also feared when he did come, because he would be walking into a trap. She hated that they were able to use her as bait to lure him into their clutches.

Escape was futile. There was always someone with her at all times, even when she bathed or went to the privy. The night before, she had tried to sneak away when she thought everyone was sleeping. She had snuck out through one of the side flaps of the tent, but apparently, the old chief could hear better than she had perceived. He found her, despite how quiet she had tried to be. He had grabbed her arm and yanked her around, demanding angrily, "Why you try leave? You stupid. You run, you die."

Was he threatening her? Margaret knew he would follow threw if she defied him again. Though she did not fear for her own life, she would not risk the life of the baby. She resolved her only option was to wait until Cort found her.

"Pardon me for asking, but how do you plan to get Maggie back? Not meaning to be the voice of doom, but there are dozens of those Indians and just the two of us."

"I have a plan."

"I am sure you do, but if you do not mind, I would like to be in on it."

"It is very simple. They took her in the first place to get me to come to them. They want me on their ground so they have the advantage. What they do not know is that Estella's mother was Indian. Her father was full Spaniard, but he married an Indian woman. Estella loved visiting her Indian side of the family, and when I married her, I went with her many times. I got to know her people and their ways. The Sioux people are quite different from the Cheyenne who have Margaret. Estella's people are kind, loving people who are honorable and good, unlike the cruel kidnappers we have to deal with now."

"Yes, they do seem to be the most horrible, debased people I have ever met. But what do the Sioux people have to do with any of this?"

"During several of my visits with Estella, some of the warriors showed me how to fight as they do. Added with my military training, I feel that I can win the fight they will definitely challenge me to when we arrive at their camp."

"I agree. You are the best fighter I have ever met. You would even beat me, I say. But what concerns me is what happens after you win. They will not let you just walk out of there."

"Actually, I believe they will. You see, as despicable as this group might be, all Indians live by a certain code of honor, something that is central to all the tribes. If someone wins a challenge fairly, then they let him go. They will honor that, and they will let Margaret go too," he said as he pulled out his gun and looked down the sights.

"All right, that is best-case scenario, but what happens if it does not go that way?"

"I have a contingency plan," Cort said as he cleaned his gun with a rag.

"Pardon?"

"Reserve, if you will." He loaded the chamber with bullets. "Estella's Sioux uncles and cousins have a debt to settle with this same group. I had one of your men deliver a message, right before we left, telling them about what has happened. If I am not mistaken, they are traveling a couple miles behind us. They will be there if we need them. I am actually betting that once the three of us get out of there, they are going to present their own challenge to them."

"My, my, you have been busy. I had no idea you had all this planned out. I am impressed."

Cort snapped the chamber shut and cocked his gun. "I am just thankful we have God on our side."

Feeling hopeful after picking up the Indians' trail again, Cort made them push their horses as hard as possible, taking as little time as possible for sleep.

"We are almost there, Randall. I can feel it. Soon we will have Margaret back home where she belongs and this will all be over."

"Yes, it will be good to get home. I do say, I am missing my wife tremendously."

"I bet you are, and with her being pregnant, you really sacrificed a lot to come with me."

"Yes, well, Maggie risked coming to France to find me. She never gave up on me, and I owe her everything."

"Soon, you will be able to tell her that yourself."

Cort looked out over the horizon and wondered what Margaret was doing right then. He constantly prayed God would protect her and keep her safe until he could rescue her. He loved her more than anything and would stop at nothing to save her.

"From what I can tell, we are less than a day's travel away from their camp. Remember the plan we discussed. You are to only be my reserve, Randall. Do not get into the middle of it, and whatever you do, do not turn your back on any of them. They will kill you first chance they get."

Randall nodded. "I just hope we are doing the right thing."

"We do not have any other choice. This is Margaret's best chance."

Randall nodded again. "Understood."

Both men sat quietly by the campfire. It would be their last night before they reached the camp.

She realized quickly as the weather changed and the sun began to blaze overhead for longer periods of time, the chief had not been threatening her as much as warning her. If she did manage to escape, she would not make it out in the sun more than a day or two. Her fair English skin would burn without coverage and cause her to die from dehydration.

So she did the only thing she could do: waited. She waited what seemed like forever for a sign, any sign that her husband was coming for her.

It was two days later, while she was sitting in the tent weaving some mats for the chief's squaw, that she heard a commotion outside. Margaret jumped to her feet and poked her head out between the flaps.

In the distance, she saw two horses galloping up with sweat-clad riders gripping their reins. Margaret put her hand over her eyes and squinted, trying to make out the faces of the cowboys approaching. Was it Cort? If it was, why didn't he bring help? There was no way the two of them could manage to get her free and all of them make it out alive. What was he thinking?

Margaret bit her lip anxiously as she saw the chief approach the horse. There was definitely something familiar about the men. The one in front dismounted first, followed by the other one. The chief was standing in the way, making it impossible for her to see if it was her husband.

CHAPTER 14

Cort and Randall arrived at the Indian camp at dusk. They had their hands on their guns as they rode in on their horses. Neither one of them let their guard down as they dismounted and stood quietly. It was obvious why they were there as they waited for the chief to come out from his tent.

Moments passed by as the two of them waited, their backs to each other, hands on their holsters.

The tent flap opened and two Indians emerged, one young and one old, followed by two squaws.

"You come, white killer of my son. I wait long time for vengeance."

Cort now understood why they had gone to such length to get him there this way. "I killed your son? Is this what this is about?"

"Yes, you kill my son when you saved Heart Full of Fire. We take her to bring you here."

"Where is she?"

"Not matter now. Now we settle blood debt."

"Yes, it does matter. I will not fight you until I know Margaret is safe."

The old chief narrowed his eyes and stared at Cort for several seconds before turning to the Indian next to him and whispering something.

The Indian went back into the tent and, after a few seconds, came back out with something. He walked forward to Cort and placed the item in his hands. Cort looked down and recognized that it was a piece of baby's clothing. In the left corner were the initials JCJ. The stitching of the lettering was unmistakably in Margaret's style. She had been teaching herself how to sew before the Indians took her. There were several other pieces of baby clothes at their home she had finished. He smiled as he thought of her doing this to keep herself busy as she waited for him.

It also gave him hope that the baby was still alive. If she was working on this, she was still pregnant. The initials also meant that she had decided on a name: James Cortland Junior, after him. She must be hoping it was a boy.

He tucked the piece of baby clothing into his pocket and looked up at the chief. "I am ready to fight. I too have a blood vengeance to settle. The warriors I killed were responsible for killing my wife and daughter. But some of them escaped. I've come to finish the job this time."

"You kill my son and many sons of this tribe. With your death, debt will be met. You fight my other son." He motioned for the man standing next to him to come forward.

"Move away, Randall. It is time to get this settled."

Cort never took his eyes off the two men in front of him as he pulled out his knife from his belt. He gripped it with ease and crouched in a fighting stance as he waited for the young warrior to make his move.

With quick and deadly precision, the warrior lashed out with a knife he had been holding behind his back.

He dodged the blade as it slashed toward him. The warrior lunged again as Cort ducked out of his way a second time.

Cort circled the Indian as he looked for an opportunity to strike back. But every time he made a move, the warrior met his blow with a defense and an attack of his own. The blow-for-blow match continued steadily until the flicker of something from the side distracted Cort just enough to allow the young Indian to thrust out and forward. Cort managed to see the glint of the knife just in time to dodge the jab that was directed to his stomach. But the Indian was trained well and quickly followed his last attack with another, and this one managed to strike across Cort's upper arm.

Cort stepped back quickly, sucking in air as he forced himself to focus past the pain. He had to win this fight. God knew what would happen to Margaret if he didn't.

Cort crouched and lunged toward his opponent, missing

him. The other man circled him, looking for an opening. From his lower position, he noticed that the young warrior had a habit of leaving his lower left side vulnerable. That was where he would attack.

Cort slashed forward and this time nicked the Indian's ribs. Without any warning, Cort quickly jumped over and landed on top of the Indian, placing his knife to his throat. "I am honored to have fought you, brave warrior."

"Kill me, white one. My life nothing after defeat."

Without another word, Cort hit the young warrior on the side of the head with his fist hard enough to knock him out. He was through taking revenge into his own hands. God had shown him that mercy was the true way of a Christian, and that when a man took his own form of revenge, he only ended up doing more damage than good. Christ showed mankind mercy, and Cort would do the same to others.

After standing up, Cort backed away slowly, still gripping his knife tightly in his right hand. "I won this fight. All of you here are witnesses. All I ask is that you return my wife to me, and then our debt will be settled."

The Indian chief stepped forward, then turned his head to the side, saying, "Bring Heart Full of Fire."

Cort eyebrows furrowed together in confusion. "Where is my wife?"

A few moments later, Margaret emerged from the tent behind the chief. Though her hair was in tangles and she was wearing Indian clothes, she looked like she was healthy.

Cort's eyes dropped to Margaret's belly. She was still visibly pregnant, and Cort signed with relief.

She rushed into her husband's arms. "I knew you would come for me," she whispered against his chest.

"I will always come for you, Margaret, until my dying breath," Cort vowed. Turning his attention to the group of Indians, he said, "You made a poor choice in taking my wife. You will regret that decision."

"Big talk, no action," the chief said smugly.

Cort backed up to his horse and jumped onto it, pulling up Margaret behind him, then he pulled his shotgun out. Keeping it pointed toward the Indians, he said to Randall, "Let's go."

As they turned and headed out toward the sunset, Cort put his fingers to his mouth and whistled loudly. As Cort, Margaret, and Randall moved south, the sounds of screams and the smell of blood followed them. It seemed Estella's people still wanted to settle their debt with her killers.

CHAPTER 15

Several days had passed and Margaret had been seen by the doctor. Though the baby seemed to be fairing well, he ordered her to remain inactive until the baby came after all she had endured.

Grateful to have an excuse to be alone, she either sat by the windowsill and looked out the window or she laid in bed resting.

She heard a faint knock at the door and a soft boy's whisper. "Mama, I know you're resting, but I want to see you, tell you I love you." There was a short pause. "I'm going now."

Margaret started to stand up, paused, and then sat back down.

What was she doing? That was her son on the other side

of the door. Though she was still shaken from her ordeal, he needed his mother and she needed him.

Margaret jumped up quickly and rushed to the door. She opened it and saw Henry's disappointed retreating figure. Hesitantly, she whispered only loud enough for him to hear, "Henry, darling, come back, please."

Pausing, he slowly turned around to make eye contact with his mother, a giant smile on his face as he said, "Mama, I'm so glad you want to see me."

Margaret felt a blush of shame cover her body. She was embarrassed, knowing that she had only just moments before actually decided to change her mind. She hated that she had hurt him.

Stepping through the door and out into the hall, Margaret replied, "Oh, my darling son, I always want to see you. Never doubt that."

A look of relief crossed Henry's face while tears welled up in his eyes. Margaret felt even more regretful that she had caused her son to doubt her love.

"Thanks, Mama," Henry said with a sheepish grin.

Margaret crossed the distance between them and gathered Henry into her arms. "You are always welcome to come and spend time with me. I love you so very much."

"I've missed you. I'm glad you're home."

"I know. I have missed you as well, and we have a lot of catching up to do."

He smiled up at his mother and nodded.

"Good, then let us get started."

This made all the hard parts of coming home worth it. She had her son back, and soon, she would get her life back —no matter what it took. Witherton had not been able to destroy her; she would not let the Indian chief have that power either.

Having Henry around made things easier for Margaret to readjust. Even though she had been away only a few months, her son had changed and matured, becoming a young boy rather than the toddler she left behind. And even though she was upset that she had missed the start of those changes, she was glad that she had managed to make it back to see the rest.

Things were not entirely different between Margaret and her brother. They had fallen right back into their old ways and were getting along just like old times. Jackie and her new baby girl were inseparable, and Margaret loved spending time with both of them.

But however smoothly things were going with the rest of her family, the situation with Cort was becoming, if anything, more troubled. Margaret did not know why, but for some reason, even though she wanted to let Cort get close to her again, something inside her kept him at a distance. She was trying so hard to let him in, but no matter how hard she tried, she only ended up putting more of a distance between them.

And it was not that Cort misunderstood what she went through. On the contrary, he did not push, he did not get angry, and he never showed her anything but love and acceptance. But even though he hid it well, Margaret knew her distancing hurt him deeply.

She wished she knew how to fix what was, or rather, what was not going on between them, but she had no clue as how to go about it.

But if Margaret was completely honest with herself, a great deal of it stemmed from the fact that she could not bring herself to let go of all the feelings that flooded her, no matter what she told herself. She felt broken from her dreadful experience, and she did not know how to communicate that to Cort.

Margaret was still lost in thought as she heard Randall and Cort talking down the hall. They must have thought her asleep.

"Randall, I have no idea how to get through to her. I have tried everything I can possibly think of and have prayed until my knees ache, yet nothing seems to make a difference. I feel like I am losing a little bit more of her each day, and I am afraid that soon, I will lose her altogether."

"Cort, I do not know what to say. I do not have any answers for what is going on with her."

"At least she doesn't have any problems with you. Why do you think that is?"

"I think that she does not fear me because I am her

brother. I do not think she knows how to open up to you at the moment."

"Do you think she blames me? If I could have gotten to her sooner, I would have, and I gladly would have laid down my life to keep her from what happened."

"She knows that, Cort, even though it might be buried deep down. She knows that you are a good man. She just needs to slay these ghosts before she can let that truth come back up to the surface."

"I suppose the only thing I can do is trust God to work things out."

"Yes. He can and He will."

"I believe that. God always makes a way."

Margaret was thinking of her past as she stared out the window, trying to make sense of what was going on in her life. She had come through so much, yet felt like she had lost so much more. She wanted to love Cort, but something was keeping her from doing it.

Did she blame him? Logically, she knew it was not his fault what happened to her, but part of her wondered if she had put up a wall without knowing it.

Then the most wonderful thing happened. From out of the blue, she remembered the conversation she had had with her father and how her father had described love.

"Love is gracious and honest. It can withstand anything and

always bears hope…. You see, love is not only a feeling but an action. Even when your heart does not feel like loving, you act it out. Emotions are fickle, and one moment you feel one way, and the next you feel completely different. But true love will act and trust that the heart will follow behind."

Her father's words rang true, even after all these years. Was God giving this to her? If she acted out love toward Cort, the feelings would have to follow. It made such perfect sense when she looked at it that way. She needed to show Cort that she still loved him, even though her heart refused to feel it right now.

Since Margaret had returned, she had not been down for dinner on doctors orders. Instead, every meal, Cort brought up a tray to her while trying to initiate a conversation. But every night, she had feigned being tired and responded with detached pleasantries.

Tonight was going to be different. *She* was going to be different. She was not going to push him away like she had been, but instead was going to make her best attempt to let him in.

When she heard the knock at the door, Margaret took a deep breath and sat up straight in bed, preparing herself to make a concerted effort to engage with her husband.

"Come in." Her voice was thick with forced cheerfulness.

Cort entered, carrying her usual tray with a meal of what appeared to be beef stew and fresh bread. The bread was no doubt sent over by Jackie as it had been for the last few months, but the soup could very well be a product of Cort's hidden talent. Apparently, somewhere along the line, he had learned to cook, and Margaret hated to admit it, but he was actually quite good at it.

With her most endearing smile, Margaret praised his hard work. "That looks delicious. I cannot wait to try it." Attempting to start a conversation, she added, "Did you make it?"

Cort raised his eyebrows in surprise. "Well, yes, actually. Sorry it is so basic, but I am limited in what I know how to make."

She gave him a sly half smirk. "I am eager to know where you learned how to cook. I have a confession to make." She paused to take a bite of the stew, closing her eyes to savor the taste. "You are a far better cook than I."

He laughed. "I hardly think so. But I will take the compliment just the same. As for where I learned, well, you will never believe this."

"Try me."

"The Royal Army trained me to be a cook, before realizing I was better suited to serve as a scout for them."

"That is it?"

"Pretty much, but I guess I was a far better cook than I thought, since I have managed to impress you."

"Indeed you have."

"Well then, that makes all those hours of slaving away over a huge hot stove in the bottom of a boat worth it, just to have this moment here with you."

Margaret eyelids fluttered, masking how his compliment manifested an uncontrollable response to want to put her wall back up.

Reminding herself that she needed to act out love, Margaret raised her eyes to meet his and whispered softly, "Thank you."

"You are most welcome."

"Cort, I… I love you."

Cort smiled at her. "I know. I have always known, no matter how it might have appeared."

"I am glad for that, then. I have been awful as of late, and I am dreadfully sorry for that."

"You do not need to apologize."

"But I do. Maybe not for you, but I do for me. You see, I need to fix what is wrong with me, and I do not know why, but I feel I need your forgiveness."

"You already have it, sweetheart. Nothing you could do will ever make me stop loving you, and with love comes forgiveness."

CHAPTER 16

*A*fter that night, Margaret and Cort's relationship slowly started on the road to healing. Their time together became less strained and more plentiful, as Margaret could be around her husband without being walled off.

Margaret was sitting by the window, sewing some baby clothes, when she felt a pain in her abdomen. Though strong, it was not sharp like the ones with Henry. It reminded her of when Sarah had told her what to expect. These felt like normal birthing pains.

"Henry, I need you to go tell your father it is time to get the doctor. The baby is coming," Margaret shouted from her room.

She stood from the window, then leaned out and braced

herself against the edge of the windowsill as another pang flashed across her body.

After the newest pain passed, she made her way over to the bed and reclined, waiting for the arrival of the doctor and Cort.

Lord, help me through this delivery. Protect me and keep the baby safe through the process. I need your strength to get through this.

The door flew open, with Cort standing on the other side. "Is the baby coming? Alfred was working with me, and he offered to go get the doctor so I could stay with you."

Margaret tried to force a smile, but was certain it came across more as a grimace. Gesturing for him to join her, she said, "I think you will have a baby by day's end."

Taking her hand in his, he whispered, "Are you ready for this?"

"As long as it's easier than my last time around, I think I can manage."

Another jab of pain crashed over her, causing her to let out a loud groan. Embarrassed, she felt her cheeks tinge with heat. "I did not expect for that to come out so loud."

"It's alright, sweetheart. You do whatever you need to." Cort's eyebrows came together. "How quick are these pains coming?"

"Why?" Margaret asked.

"I heard somewhere that the closer the pains together, the sooner the baby will arrive."

"Oh, that makes sense. I did not know that since my last birthing experience was difficult to say the least." Worry began to take a hold of Margaret's heart. "I need you to know, when I gave birth to Henry, we both nearly died. The doctor insisted I should be able to have more children with no complications. However, if the worst should happen, I want you to promise to save the baby."

"Stop that," Cort ordered. "We aren't going to talk like that. You're both going to be fine."

Margaret inhaled sharply as a fresh pain took hold.

"I think I should check and see what is going on."

"No, we can wait for the doctor," Margaret insisted.

Cort came around and gingerly lifted the edge of Margaret's skirt. Shaking his head, he stated, "I don't think we can. I see the baby's head."

Five pushes later, and Cort was holding a plump, baby girl in his arms.

"I cannot believe you just delivered our daughter," Margaret said with awe.

"Do you want to hold her?"

"Yes, please, more than anything."

Cort handed the perfect creature to Margaret. She was adorable with her whisps of black hair on top of her head and hazel eyes starring back at Margaret. The baby's soft coos were like salve to her heart. She knew everything she had gone through brought her to this moment.

A soft knock came at the door. "Can I come in?" Henry asked from the other side.

"Of course. We want you to meet your baby sister," Cort stated with pride.

Henry entered the room as a large grin formed on his face. "I guess this makes me a big brother."

"It sure does, Henry," Cort confirmed as he patted his eldest son on the back. "And I know you are going to be the best one ever."

"You mean other than me?" Randall jested from the door.

"Pish-posh, you are only older by three minutes, Rand," Margaret playfully admonished back. "How did you hear about the baby?"

"I was out working on the fence line by the main road when I saw Alfred galloping by with a frantic look on his face. I knew it must mean the baby was coming so I loaded up Jackie and the baby in the wagon and we came over."

"Where is my dear friend, anyway?" Margaret inquired.

"Right here," Jackie said as she entered the room with her infant daughter in her arms. Sitting down beside her friend on the edge of the bed, she added, "We are so happy for you both."

The baby's cooing was interrupted by a small cry. "I think the baby is getting hungry," Margaret explained. "I think I should feed her."

"Before we go, have you decided on a name?" Randall asked with curiosity.

Margaret looked at Cort who nodded for her to go ahead and reveal the baby's name. "Susan Marie, after Cort's mother."

CHAPTER 17

Margaret had started to work again, taking charge of the household and putting things back in order. Everything had gone into chaos while she was gone and even after while she was forced to rest for the baby's sake. Their home was in disarray, and she wanted to fix it.

As Margaret finished up her chores in the kitchen while the baby napped, Jackie arrived. She had taken it upon herself to stop by every few days to "bring Margaret the local town news," knowing Margaret still did not want to go into town and face all the questions about her abduction.

They talked about the work their husbands were doing. Apparently, Randall had decided to go into the wheat business—due to a tip from a local farmer that a need for wheat was on the rise. According to Jackie, their crops were doing exceptionally well and they were looking forward to a rich harvest.

Their daughter, whom they named Charlotte Elaine after Margaret and Randall's mother, was healthy and just learning to crawl.

Smiling, Margaret said, "Charlotte really takes after her father. She has Rand's eyes."

Margaret watched her niece inch across the floor. Moving slower than she wished, she would get frustrated, roll over and play with her hands for a few minutes, then flip back over and start the pattern again.

Laughing, Jackie said, "I know. She has his spirit too. She is already causing trouble, trying to get into anything she can manage."

Margaret joked, "I do not think my brother is completely to blame for that. Do not forget, you have more than your share of 'spirit' as well."

Jackie sniffed, putting on airs as if she were offended. "You think you are so very smart. Well, you are not."

Margaret snickered. "Possibly, but I know the both of you, and I have never met two people who cause more trouble, which proves my point."

Jackie shrugged. "Perhaps you are right. I suppose that is why I love Randy so much. He reminds me of myself."

"I know from experience that Rand is very much the same way," Margaret said, thinking back to when she first found her brother.

"Henry seems to be sprouting up overnight."

"Yes, I know. I hardly can believe it myself." Then Margaret added without thinking, "Every day I see more of Henry in him."

"There are definite features that are not yours, like his chin for instance. It sticks out much further than yours. Also, his hair is blond, and his eyes are brown."

Margaret stiffened, knowing that Henry did not look like her. She dreaded the day he asked why that was, and she had to explain their past to him.

Not noticing Margaret's discomfort, Jackie continued, "Does Henry know about his birth father? Have you ever discussed him or your life before you left England?"

Margaret shifted in her seat and avoided answering the question directly. "It is still difficult for me to talk about him or that time in my life. Of course, it seems to pale in comparison on a scale of bad as opposed to what I have gone through since then. But for some reason, what happened with Henry hurts in a way that is much worse."

"Maybe because what happened to you back then occurred by the hands of people close to you rather than strangers."

Margaret did not voice her agreement. After several moments of silence, she stated in a monotone voice, "Those who are closest to you have the ability to hurt you the deepest."

"If you do not mind me asking, did you love the duke? I mean, before he did what he did to you."

"I thought I did. But I realize now I was very naive and

had no clue as to what true love was. My father was right in that respect. Perhaps, if I had listened to him rather than my own stubborn desires, the duke would not have had the opportunity to do what he did and it would not have cost my husband his life. But as for loving him, I did not, not really—not in any way that counted. But I do know I loved Henry and I also loved Michel. Part of me still does.

"I never knew I would have three great loves in my life, ending with the love of my life. Cort lets me in completely and loves my independent nature. He wants me to work with him—we are partners in every sense of the word. He wants me to be involved with the ranch and the horses, and that means the world to me. All the things that my father said love is, Cort embodies. He is patient, kind, selfless, and honest. He persevered and was steadfast in his love for me even when I did not respond in return. I still marvel at how lucky I am to have him in my life."

"Luck has nothing to do with it, chéri. You are blessed by God."

Margaret nodded. "I know I am."

CHAPTER 18

Randall and Jackie, along with Charlotte, went every Sunday to church with Cort, but Margaret still did not want to go into town and face everyone's prying. She opted to read her Bible at home instead. Henry stayed with her, keeping her company.

Then something unexpected happened. Henry asked if he could go with his father to church.

"Mama, I like being with you on Sunday mornings, but I want to start going to church with the rest of the family. Is it okay if I go?"

Happily, she gave her permission. "I think that would be wonderful."

"Would you want to come with us this next Sunday?"

Margaret thought about it and realized she did not want to miss out on being with her family. She would brave town for her son's sake, and secretly, she did miss hearing Pastor Thompson's sermons. "I think that would be nice."

"I'm glad to hear it, Mama."

Later that evening, after dinner and nightly chores, Margaret and Cort made their way to their room.

"Why don't you get in bed, I'm going to sit by the window and say my nightly prayers first."

Margaret nodded and headed toward their bed.

Cort sat down on the bench and waited several seconds with his eyes closed before starting.

"God, you know my heart and how I wish to please you. Give me the right words to say to those around me. More specifically, I pray that you heal my wife. All I want is for her to find true healing from her past—and that can only be done through you.

"Lord, I thank you that my son has found you and wants to know you. The day I prayed with him and he accepted you, Jesus, was one of the happiest days of my life.

"I thank you that Jackie and Randall know you, Lord. Father, I ask that you protect my family. Send angels to be with them and keep them safe. Give them peace and help me to express your love to them each day.

"Bless my ranch and put your hand over it. I give it over to you, since it all is yours to begin with, Lord. I thank you for providing for my family. Give us all a good night's rest and help me to be a good witness for you. I love you, Lord. Thank you for saving me and changing me into a better person a little each day. Amen."

"No, no, not him too. Nooooo. Please, oh no, no—" Margaret sat bolt upright in bed, heaving sobs of fear.

Reflexively, Cort sat up and reached over to gather her into his arms, whispering words of comfort and love.

The dream had come again. It was the same every time.

A man she could not make out knocked her to the ground. Cort was a few feet from her and she was trying to reach out to him, but before she could, the other man stepped in between them.

Hearing the voice of the other man, she tried to make out what he was saying, but it was muffled.

Fear overwhelmed her as she tried to get up to help Cort. She knew the man between them wanted to kill him. She could hear the hate in the tone of his voice.

When she heard a gunshot, Margaret screamed, and then darkness enveloped her.

After several minutes, she finally calmed down enough to realize that someone was with her. Recognizing Cort, she grabbed at him, patting to make sure he was really there.

"You *are* here," she said as she tried to catch her breath. "You are truly here. Thank goodness, I thought…. I was so afraid that you were…. I do not know what I would have done if you were…."

She tried to swallow away the dryness in her mouth but was unable. It felt as if it consisted of fear itself and was choking her.

"Yes, sweetheart, I'm here, and I will never leave you. Do not worry, you are safe."

Resting her head on his shoulder, she whispered, "It is not me that I am frightened for. It is you."

He pulled back slightly and looked into her eyes with confidence. "Nothing is going to happen to me. I promise you that."

"But he is so much more powerful than you. I felt it in the dream."

"Who is *he*?"

"I believe the man in my dream is… the duke."

Margaret felt him tense. "And in your dream, what happened?"

"It is all so foggy. It seems so hard to remember now, but it was so real while it was happening. It felt so real, and I was so sure…. I truly believed you had been…." She could not finish the thought. It scared her too much to think of Cort dying.

"It was only a dream, and I am here with you. That is all that matters. I love you, Margaret. With every breath of my being and every fiber in my body, I love you."

CHAPTER 19

Since hearing Cort's prayer the other night, Margaret had been searching to find what could help her heal. She believed doing something she loved would help her let go of what was troubling her, and working with horses came first to mind.

Margaret made her way out to the corral where Cort was working on breaking a new horse. He had purchased it in hopes to breed into their existing bloodline.

When she thought about it, she realized she had done herself a disservice by allowing Cort to run the horse farm so long without her being involved. It had been her dream, even before she met Cort, and when they had gotten married, it had become their dream together. It was about time she took control and started making her own dreams come to pass. And that meant finding the perfect stallion to sire a colt for Charlie. Margaret considered using Chester, but for some reason, she did not think he would produce the best colt. She would just have to look elsewhere.

Hopping up onto one of the bottom wooden slats of the corral, she swung her arms on top and rested her chin in her hands as she watched Cort work with the new horse.

He was so submerged in his connection with the stallion, he had not yet noticed her nearby. She watched her husband, liking the idea that she could observe him without him knowing it.

Cort moved in a circle, leading the horse with a halter rope that spanned the ten feet between them. The stallion, in turn, circled him as he galloped along the corral wall. The way they moved together was like a dance. Margaret could see the muscles smoothly roll beneath both their skins in union. And even though Cort had a whip in his hand, it seemed as if he did not need it. It was as if the stallion could sense what Cort was feeling and was naturally obeying his every command.

Margaret marveled at her husband's ability. She could hardly believe that this horse before her was the same one that Cort had bought only four days ago—completely wild.

She had to admit he had a gift, a special touch that she had never seen anyone else possess. Rather than break the horse's spirit, he bent the stallion's will to match his own. She was even a little envious of how natural it came to him.

After a few more minutes of Cort giving various signals with the rope, Margaret noticed a slight tightening in his wrist as he slowed the stallion down to a trot, then a canter, and finally a dead stop.

He approached the horse and began to pat him down while speaking soft words Margaret could not make out. She interrupted, saying, "I want to be involved with the horses, Cort. I can do it when the baby is napping and we can also take turns working out here. I think it is time I start being a part of our dreams for this place."

Cort turned his head quickly, startled to have company. Henry had started school a month earlier.

His eyebrows shot up in surprise. "I would love you to work with me. These horses belong to you as much as they do to me."

Margaret gave him a grateful smile and looked longingly at the horse. One of her secret hopes in coming to the Americas was being able to break a wild horse. She had never seen one and had only heard stories. Yet there stood one—most possibly the most beautiful horse she had ever seen.

He had faultless lines and markings. He was absolutely perfect… and that meant he was perfect for Charlie. He would be the perfect horse to sire a colt for her. But first, he had to be completely broken.

"Could I?" She pointed to herself and then the horse.

He paused a moment, appearing worried, then motioned her over to the gate. "Sure, come on in. I will give you your first lesson in breaking horses."

Margaret entered the corral nervously. It had seemed

like a good idea before she had actually gone in, but now the impressive beast loomed right before her and she was not quite sure she could hold her ground with the wild stallion.

Reading her doubts, he said, "Do not worry, Margaret. I am right here and I have broken plenty of horses. I will not let anything happen to you."

He gently put his hands on her shoulders and turned her around so that her back fit into the curve of his body. Taking her hand in his own, he put it up to the horse's nose, allowing him to take in her scent and lack of fear or threat.

After a few seconds, Cort put the rope in his wife's hand and led her to the middle of the corral, the rope tightening as they went.

And then Margaret became part of the dance. She felt the power move between her and the stallion as the wind whipped through her hair. She felt the firm guidance of her husband behind her—supporting her, yet allowing her to take control as they turned in circles. And Margaret felt peace for the first time in a long time as she danced the dance.

The months flew by as Margaret and Cort worked with the horses, and peace and love began to flow more freely from Margaret.

Charlie was with foal, the father being the wild stallion

they had broken—named Two Rifles after what Cort traded the Indians for him.

It was Charlotte's first birthday and no set of parents could be bursting with more parental pride than Randall and Jackie. They had decided to throw a party in honor of the occasion, and Margaret was running late getting everything ready to leave for the celebration.

She yelled down the hall to Henry's room, "Henry, darling, hurry up. We do not want to be late. Aunt Jackie will be very unsettled if we do not get there on time."

She heard the scuttle of feet rush down the hall and then witnessed a blurring streak pass by, heading straight for the door.

"Stop. Turn." Margaret commanded, waiting to go over her son's appearance. He braked and, with an annoyed spin, twisted around, fidgeting while waiting for his mother's inspection.

As she took in his appearance, she noted the dress pants she had made him only two months before were now barely passable for social occasions, scarcely reaching the top of his shoes. He was growing so fast, and though he was only approaching his sixth birthday, and had been relatively small when he was younger, he had grown nearly three inches in a matter of mere months.

Henry's growth spurts were also affecting his shirts, his current one being no exception, only just managing to touch his wrists when his arms were fully extended. Luckily, his shoes were holding out, since Margaret had purposely bought them a size too big, using socks to compensate for the size difference until they fit.

"All right, you look presentable." He gave her a large grin and started to turn away, but Margaret said, "Hold one moment, please."

She covered the distance between them and licked her fingers lightly, using them to comb his hair into place. Then, almost as an afterthought, she added, "Hold out your hands."

Reluctantly, he put out his hands, but with the fingers bent at the end. Margaret knew that trick from her brother when they had been little.

"Extend your fingers all the way."

Grudgingly, he obeyed, and Margaret recognized the unmistakable dirt under his fingernails.

"Oh no, you do not. You are not going over there with your hands looking like that. Go wash them up before we leave."

"Ahhh, Mother, I—" Recently, Henry had taken from calling her "mama" to "mother." Though to most, the change would be small, to her it was one more sign her son was growing up.

"Do not 'Mother' me. Go wash up."

Knowing how far he could push his mother before she got angry, he unenthusiastically made his way to the washbasin by the kitchen.

Realizing that Cort had not yet made it in from the corral, Margaret stepped out onto the porch and scanned the terrain for him. Where was that man? He always seemed to get preoccupied with his work and would accidentally neglect their social engagements.

She spotted him rushing toward the homestead. He gave her a small smile as he walked in. "I am sorry I am not ready to go, but I was trying to familiarize Chester with one of the new mares."

As he strode past her through the doorway, Margaret was inundated with the masculine smell of leather and sweat—the essential elements she associated with a man—and she was quickly taken over by a deep desire to touch him, to reach out and pull him near.

But as quickly as it came, it passed, and Margaret was left feeling a sudden pang of loss. She wanted to smell him again, to feel the quick moment of intimacy—so uncomplicated by their normal reactions of hesitancies and expectation when they were alone.

She followed him to the back room, stopping only momentarily to tell Henry to go hitch up the wagon.

Margaret entered the room, catching Cort in the act of undressing. Hurrying to try to change his shirt quickly, Cort did not notice Margaret at the door watching.

She studied him while he unbuttoned his shirt and took in his truly mannish form. He was handsome, but not like the men she had known in Europe. His body was hard and tough from working outdoors.

As he worked at putting on his fresh shirt, his muscles moved fluidly underneath his steady hands.

Margaret moved toward him. She did not know what came over her, but suddenly, she found herself sliding in between her husband and the dresser.

Startled by her sudden appearance and close proximity, Cort took in a deep breath and held it. He stammered out, "W-what are you doing?"

Not knowing how to answer, she realized she did not want to answer. Instead, she leaned up and took possession of his lips with her own.

At first, Cort stood there, rooted to the spot by shock. But after a moment's hesitation, he reached down and gently placed his hand on the side of her cheek. He slipped his other arm around her waist and drew her close.

Margaret leaned into his touch, clinging to her sheer need for him. Nothing else mattered but letting him know how much she loved him.

Cort brushed her hair back and tucked it behind her ear gently. "I love you, Margaret."

"I love you too." Then she winked, adding, "Now hurry up and kiss me again."

CHAPTER 20

They arrived at the celebration a half hour late. But once Jackie saw the smile on her best friend's face, no rebukes followed. Instead, when Jackie was able to find a few free moments, she pulled Margaret into her bedroom, away from the other guests. "So tell me, chéri, what happened between the two of you? I do so know *that* smile."

Margaret knew she exuded happiness and was ecstatic to tell her friend why. "Oh, Jackie, it was so wonderful." Her eyebrows shot up in excitement. "I think Cort and I finally turned a corner."

Jackie smiled. "I am so glad to hear that, chéri. We are lucky to have the men we do." Astutely, Jackie added, "You know the reason why both Randy and Cort put their wives first, do you not?"

Margaret's eyebrows came together in a line of puzzlement. "I have no idea."

"It is simple, chéri. God's love made them that way. Both Randy and Cort manifest God's love in all they do. They know only through allowing God's love to flow through them can they truly be the best husbands and fathers. I have seen such a profound change in Randy since he has come to know the Lord. He no longer uses the pleasures of this world to fill the void in his life."

"That is true. My father was a wonderful example of Godly love."

Jackie nodded. "You told me about your father and how he was a wonderful father. He actively sought God in his life, did he not?"

"Yes, my father read his Bible, prayed twice a day, went to church—everything a Christian is supposed to do."

"You see, he had the example of Christ as well, and I suspect he most likely was a marvelous husband when your mother was alive."

"Yes, he most definitely was that. Everyone said so."

Jackie asserted, "Perfect love only comes from a fountainhead of perfect love. God *is* that fountainhead, and only He can give us the capability to love perfectly."

"Jackie, my dear sister, I love that we can have these conversations now. I feel even more close to you because we finally share the same faith."

Margaret's favorite moment of Charlotte's first birthday celebration was when she took a piece of cake and smashed it in her father's face when he bent down to kiss her after singing "Happy Birthday." The look of sheer astonishment on Randall's face was priceless. Charlotte appeared angelic, with her golden blonde hair and violet eyes, but she was every bit as mischievous as her parents ever were in their prime.

Margaret and Cort decided to stay on after all the other guests left to help clean up. Randall, Cort, and Henry were cleaning outside while Margaret and Jackie cleaned inside.

"This was a nice celebration, but now Henry is going to want one for his sixth birthday next month and it, of course, is going to have to outdo this since he is older."

Jackie laughed as she wiped dry a serving platter. "Well, you can count on me for all the advice and help you need."

Henry interrupted their conversation, bringing in a half-full container of sugar, which had been placed outside for the drinks. Margaret watched as her son darted his head side to side, scanning the room, and then asked, "Aunt Jackie, where do you want me to set this?"

Jackie smiled at him. "Place it over on the table, but out of Charlotte's reach."

He nodded and put the sugar dish down, then ran out of the room with Margaret yelling to his retreating figure, "Do not run in the house. You know the rules apply everywhere."

Jackie walked over to the pantry with the serving platter

and disappeared into the tiny closet. From across the kitchen, Margaret heard a soft groan, followed by a gasp coming from the pantry. Worried, Margaret put down the glass she was cleaning and rushed toward pantry. She found Jackie bent down on one knee, doubled over in pain.

"What is the matter?"

"Nothing, I am all right."

Jackie tried to stand up but was visibly shaking and quickly fell back down to her knee. Margaret put one of Jackie's arms around her shoulder to support her sister-in-law's weight, helping her over to the kitchen table.

Jackie sat in one of the breakfast nook chairs while Margaret dampened a fresh towel and then handed it to her.

"Are you going to tell me why you almost fainted a moment ago?"

"I just overexerted myself. We were going to tell you and Cort in a few weeks, because it is still so early."

Margaret asked hesitantly, "What is too early?"

"To tell you about our new baby."

She had not expected Jackie to announce she was pregnant with her second child, yet was happy to hear she would be having another niece or nephew.

"That's fantastic," Margaret replied with a smile.

"I know. We were not even trying."

"So much has changed. I cannot believe all we have gone through. You both deserve to be happy," Margaret stated.

"Are you wanting another?" Jackie inquired.

Margaret nodded. "I love being pregnant and would still love to give Cort a little boy."

"Yes, well, it will happen soon enough. You have only been home for little less than a year, and Susan isn't even one yet."

Just as Margaret was about to reply, Randall, Cort, and Henry walked into the kitchen, each with a stack of plates.

"So Rand, when were you going to share your great news with your dear sister?" Margaret asked.

Randall shot his wife a look of surprise, then, after a moment's hesitation, replied, "Why, it seems someone beat me to it. As it happens, I had planned to tell you tonight."

"You were, were you, Randy? I thought we had discussed we were waiting," Jackie said with irritation.

"No, you decided and informed me it was going to be that way. I, on the other hand, had every intention of telling my sister as soon as possible."

"Randall, you very well know that is not true."

"Truly? I daresay, I think you had better say that to keep me from whipping you," Margaret teased.

"You? Whip me? I do not think so, my dear *little* sister."

"Little… ha. By only three minutes."

"All right, you three, enough quarreling. We can resume this later and place wagers on who will win the fight," Cort baited. "But for now, will one of you tell Henry and me what the big news is that you are fighting over?"

Margaret shrugged, saying, "I think Randall and Jackie should be the ones to share it."

Jackie nodded to her husband, deferring to him.

"Well, it seems that Jackie and I… are expecting a new baby."

"That *is* great news. Congratulations to the both of you."

Randall walked over to his wife and wrapped his arm around her shoulders. They made such a perfect couple with his dark hair and blue eyes set off by her strawberry blonde hair and smoldering green eyes. But what really made the picture complete was the look of sheer happiness and joy on both of their faces.

"I think we should be on our way. We have"—Margaret nodded to everyone and then put her attention back on her husband—"have an early morning tomorrow."

"That is right." Randall smacked the side of his head with the palm of his hand in jest. "I almost forgot tomorrow is Sunday. We have been so busy getting everything ready for today." Randall shot Cort a charming grin—one that was a perfect match to the one Margaret used to use to get her way. "You would not mind giving a ride to your dear brother- and sister-in-law, now would you?"

"No, of course not. We will be by at half past seven to pick you up."

Randall winked at his nephew. "If you are good, I will let you hold your cousin on the way."

Trying to act the part of a man, Henry shrugged. "If it will help you out, Uncle Randy."

"Well, if you do not want to…," he said.

Henry rushed to assure him. "No, I want to. Susan only wants to be held by mother."

"Thanks, you are a big help. I do not see how I would get by without you—or your father, for that matter."

"The pleasure is all ours. We love going to church with the lot of you," Cort said, before they headed out the door to go home.

CHAPTER 21

Cort patted the neck of a full-term filly, saying, "It has been a hard few months, getting through the winter and making sure the mares don't lose their foals. But it's going to be worth it."

Stepping out of the stall, he wrapped his arm around his wife's waist, and led her out of the stables. They walked behind the structure and over to a nearby clearing where Cort sat, patting a spot on the grass next to him. Since they were both in work clothes, Margaret did not have to worry about getting dirty.

She joined her husband and sighed in contentment. "I have to say, I am quite pleased with the progress we have made. Not many horse breeders can say they have three new colts their first season, especially with the bloodlines we are sporting. We are doing a fine job rearing some horses around here." The words sounded silly to Margaret's ears as she said them. She had planned to speak like a horse rancher, but instead, the words felt foreign on her tongue.

Cort shook his head in amusement and tried to stifle a laugh, but he was unsuccessful. "What? What is so humorous, James Cortland Westcott?"

"Nothing," he said, trying to keep himself from doubling over in laughter. "Nothing at all."

She sniffed, pouting over the fact he was amused at her expense. "I swear, every now and then, you act such the opposite of your upbringing as an Englishman. Truly, at this moment, you seem the very brutish Yank cowboy I distaste so venomously."

Indignant, she stood up, preparing herself to walk away, but Cort grabbed her arm and gently pulled her down beside him.

In a light voice, Cort said, "Come on, Margaret, you know I am only joking around. I did not mean any harm by it. You should hear how adorable you sound when you try to talk the lingo of a cowboy. Every time you do, your lovely English accent comes bursting right through." He put his hand on the side of her face, and then added in a serious tone, "If I did hurt you by my amusement, I am sorry. You know I never want to hurt you, do you not?"

After a moment's hesitation, Margaret gave him a half smile. "Yes, I know that."

"Good, and do not forget it, or how much I love you

either." Then Cort grabbed Margaret and planted a kiss on her lips.

Margaret kissed him back, wrapping her arms around his neck.

Cort kissed her cheek as he whispered in her ear, "Did I tell you how much I love working with you?"

"I think you are about to show me," Margaret stated with a knowing smile.

It was a beautiful day to be living in the Colorado Territory. The sun was high in the luminous, blue sky, the flowers were in full bloom, and the warmth was just right as Margaret and Cort sat on a blanket in a meadow near their ranch.

"I am glad we decided to go on this picnic with Henry and Susan. They have both been exceptionally good lately. They deserve to have a treat."

"*We* deserve it," Cort corrected.

"You are right. We all do." Margaret watched as Henry raced around, trying to catch frogs, which, at the moment, were getting the best of him. Susan was toddling after him, trying to keep up.

"I cannot believe how much energy they both have." She winked at Cort, adding, "They must get it from their father."

Cort chuckled. "I don't know. Their mother seems to have a lot too." He leaned forward and kissed her softly.

"I have something I want to tell you," Margaret confessed. "I just found out myself, and I wanted the moment to be right." She brushed her hand along the side of his face and down his arm until her hand reach his and she took it into her own. "And I think it is."

He smiled at her and waited for her to continue.

She swallowed a couple of times, buying herself a few seconds to get her nerves under control. "I want to try for another child."

When Cort sat still for several moments, Margaret poked him lightly with her free hand. "Did you hear me? I said I want another baby." She paused. "Do you not feel the same?"

"I wasn't sure if you would want more children. We have two after all, a boy and a girl."

Margaret smiled. "I have always wanted lots of children. My dream was to raise babies and horses on a farm one day. We seem to be doing good on the horse end; we need to just catch up on the baby end now."

Cort frowned. "The truth be told, Margaret, I am scared. I am scared to death that I will not be capable of being the father our children deserve. It's always in the back of my mind, the fear I will not be able to protect our children."

Margaret slowly turned back around and brushed a strand of hair out of her face as she probed her husband with a questioning look. "But whatever would give you that idea? You are absolutely perfect with Henry and Susan, and I know you will be the same with a new baby."

He lowered his shoulders in defeat. "I love Henry and Susan, and I try to do right by them, but I wake up every day fearful something will happen to one of them that I could have prevented—but did not. It scares me, the idea of bringing another child into this world—a world I have no control over how it treats the ones I love—it is hard."

Margaret understood perfectly. He sounded exactly like she did when she tried to comprehend why things were as they were in the world. But it troubled her that Cort was talking that way. He always seemed to be so confident in his responsibilities, and this sounded as if he doubted himself capable of being a good father, and she already knew he was whenever she watched Henry or Susan look at Cort with love and admiration.

"You are a good man, Cortland Westcott. I have told you that before when you needed to hear it, and I am telling you again. You *are* a good man, a wonderful husband, and a faultless father." She reached up and touched the side of his face. "Trust me on this. I would never lie to you."

Cort continued to stare out into the distance over Margaret's shoulder, answering only after several moments of silence. "When I put Polly into the ground next to her mother and heaved the dirt onto her tiny casket, a piece of me was buried with her, and I knew I would never be able to look at the world or myself the same way again. I know no man is perfect and things happen that are impossible for us to make sense of, even with the help of God. And I know we will love our children, all of them, and protect them with every last breath we possess, but I still wake up in the night sometimes, terrified that Henry or Susan will one day meet the same fate as Polly."

Margaret realized that the only way to get through to Cort and really make him see it would be all right was by bringing into the conversation the one thing he could not dispute.

"I wonder, where is your God now?"

Jolted back to the present, away from his haunting memories, Cort leveled his gaze to meet his wife's and said with a sudden passion, "*My* God?" Then, as if he pondered her query, he paused for several seconds before replying with a sudden burst of confidence. "My God is with me always and protects those I love when I cannot do it myself."

Margaret smiled brightly and winked at him playfully. "That is more like it. Now you are sounding like the faith-filled cowboy I married."

He chuckled. "Yes, thank you for the shove in the right direction. I needed it." He reached out and put his hands on either side of Margaret's face. "I think another baby sounds wonderful."

CHAPTER 22

She made her way onto the porch of their home and sat down on one of the rocking chairs. She looked out on the beautiful landscape of Colorado and marveled at the gorgeous sunset, which made the mountains appear majestic as the sky swirled with gorgeous shades of pink, purple, and orange around them. The breathtaking scenery reminded her of the most perfectly painted picture.

In that moment, Margaret knew what she had to do. It was time for her to give her life to Jesus fully and to hold nothing back. She wanted more than anything to know the peace her family did and have the confidence to trust the Lord with all her heart. Only then, would she feel true peace regarding her past.

Remembering how Cort would pray to God, Margaret said, "Dear Lord, as I sit here in the twilight you have shaped, I am reminded of how you created everything, even this moment, in which you cared enough for me to design something so wondrous. But not only have you made this picturesque view for me, you have blessed me with a loving family. You have been patient with me, giving me grace, even when I have not deserved it. I know you love me, you have always loved me, but I have been selfish and allowed my circumstances to dictate my feelings. God, please forgive me. I know you have kept me alive, you saved my son and daughter as well as my husband and brother. Help me to give the pain from my past to you and help me to not dwell on my losses but reflect on my blessings. I realize now, I have always prayed to you with a list of demands, but I have never asked your will for my life. I have never given control over to you, and I know now, I will never find true contentment until I do. Lord, I relinquish control of my life to you."

Tears of joy fell from Margaret's eyes as she finally felt true freedom in the Lord. She no longer felt burdened by her past or worried about the future. An immense relief flooded her heart, and she was finally unencumbered by completely giving her whole life to God.

The next Sunday morning, Margaret cooked breakfast for her family as Cort and Henry finished their morning chores. She could not wait to go to church with her family.

She heard the approaching footsteps from the hall and smiled to herself. It was going to be a glorious day indeed.

Cort came up behind Margaret and nibbled lightly on her neck before giving her a quick hug around the waist with one arm while sneaking a piece of bacon from the platter beside her with his other hand, which he promptly popped into his mouth. "Delicious, sweetheart."

Playfully, she smacked his hand. "You need to wait until breakfast, Cort."

He chuckled. "If you insist. I suppose I can wait a little longer."

He sat down at the breakfast table and, as if on cue, asked, "You ready for church this morning?"

Margaret brought the platter of eggs and bacon over to the table and placed it beside the toasted bread and fresh coffee, which already sat on top of it. "Indeed I am."

A giant grin crossed Cort's face as he said, "There seems to be a new glow about you? Are you pregnant again?"

Laughing as she shook her head, she replied, "No, the glow you are seeing is my happiness from giving my past over to God."

"I am so glad, Margaret. You have no idea. I have been praying for this since you returned to us." Then he looked at her skeptically. "I am sorry for bringing *that* up."

Margaret patted his arm lightly. "It is all right, Cort. You no longer have to worry about upsetting me. I have come to peace with what happened to me. I have given all of it over to God, and He has taken my burdens from me."

He lifted her up by the waist and swung her around and around in the kitchen, causing both of them to laugh.

"I am so happy, sweetheart. This is the best news I have ever heard."

Henry came into the room, holding Susan in his arms. He looked at both of them as if they had gone senseless. "What is going on, Father, Mother?"

"I have wonderful news, Henry."

"Is it about wanting to have another baby? I already know."

She shook her head. "No, it is not about that. Although, we should probably discuss how you are aware of that since we have not told anyone about it. Have you been listening in on private conversations?"

Henry blushed from embarrassment and looked away.

"Enough of that. Today is too happy a day to ruin with such talk. I am celebrating the freedom I have found in the Lord."

Henry's eyebrows shot up in excited surprise. "Truly, Mother?"

"Yes, my darling, my faith in God is finally complete. I have given my past over to God."

"I am so happy to hear that," Henry exclaimed.

"I am sorry it has taken me this long to do it."

"It is all right, Mother. All that matters is that you have."

And he was right. It did not matter when but only that she did.

When Margaret and her family walked into the newly built Congregational Church of Boulder Valley, all eyes turned to them. The church had only a handful or regular attendees, including Randall's family and four others.

Randall and Jackie rushed up to them and took turns hugging Margaret. "Mags, I am so glad you decided to come today," Randall said.

Jackie reached out and squeezed her friend's hand. "You should come sit with us."

Margaret nodded and allowed them to guide her over to the front pew.

Pastor Thompson made his way over to them and said, "It is so good to see your *whole* family here today."

"I am glad to be here, Pastor," Margaret said.

After the other families came and made their introductions to Margaret, everyone took their seats and Pastor Thompson began his service.

"Friends, we are gathered here today and I feel led by the Holy Spirit to teach on love this morning."

Margaret felt herself tense with excitement. It seemed every time a pivotal moment in her relationship with God manifested, He would have a sermon about love waiting for her to hear.

"We are all bonded together through God's unconditional love. It links us together in genuineness and unity. We are called not to love with only words but by our deeds. Our actions will show the world who we serve and who has poured out His merciful grace upon us. Grace that heals us, grace that frees us, grace that completes us. We love God because He first loved us, and that love is all we will ever need. It will carry us through difficult times and sustain us when we are weak. It casts out all fear."

Pastor Thompson's words confirmed everything Margaret had come to understand over the past couple of days. She knew she was changed forever because she had surrendered herself to her destiny as a child of God.

After service, Jackie asked Margaret and Cort to come over for dinner. They wanted to celebrate.

As they sat around the dinner table, Margaret felt it would be the perfect time to tell her brother and best friend about their additional good news.

Jackie had really found she had a talent for cooking and was quite adept at making fried chicken with mashed potatoes and gravy. She also had prepared fresh corn on the cob from their most recent crop, along with a homemade peach pie from their orchard.

Margaret helped set the table with dishes and eating utensils and poured glasses of iced tea for each of them while Jackie placed the platters of food in the center.

"I am so happy you decided to rededicate your life to God, Maggie. It was hard when I felt we could not talk about it without upsetting you. My relationship with the Lord has become the most important part of my life. I feel like such a different person because of it."

"I know what you mean. I feel so light now that I have given God control of my life. The pressure of trying to do everything myself is gone."

As they sat down around the table, Margaret lovingly looked around at her family. Henry was sitting with Charlotte and Susan both in his lap, in between his uncle and father, and Jackie was next to Randall. Everyone had enormous smiles on their faces, and Margaret was grateful for all her good fortune.

"Let us all join hands together as we pray over the meal." Randall waited for everyone to do as requested, then continued after everyone's heads were bowed and eyes were closed. "Dear Lord, thank you for this day you have given us, for the food you have provided, and the family with whom we share it. Amen."

Margaret squeezed Cort's leg under the table and looked at him, relaying her desire to tell everyone about their pregnancy. Cort nodded. "Everyone, we have some fantastic news."

"More good news? I say, I think we will not be able to handle it," Randall jested.

"I promise this is the last of it."

"Randy, stop teasing your sister," Jackie chastised her husband. "Go ahead and continue, Maggie."

"Cort and I have decided that we want to start trying for another child."

Jackie clasped her hands together and exclaimed, "Oh, chéri, that is such wonderful news. We are so happy for you."

Randall said, "Wonderful news. Today is truly a great day indeed."

Cort looked over at Margaret with a tender expression. "We are fortunate beyond all measure."

CHAPTER 23

Lord and Lady York were throwing a ball, an uncommon occurrence in the territory, in honor of their grandson coming to America after attending university in France. Margaret had not been to a ball since crossing the Atlantic, and she had not danced since France.

The night was going to be simply fabulous. She was wearing one of her dresses that she had brought over from France, and since the West was almost two years behind with fashion, the dress was barely out of style.

It was in a shade of deep blue, the under-slip consisting of a rich mixture of satin and silk. The top layer was chiffon that had gold that wove in and out of the material. The bodice had to be let out a smidge in order to accommodate for her body's changes after having her second child. A row of tiny embroidered gold flowers trimmed the edges of the top and sleeves, and her feet were graced with golden slippers.

Drops of diamonds and gold hung on each ear with a matching necklace—a gift from Cort after the sale of their first colt. Her hair was done in an up-twist with gold threads of lace woven in and out of her raven locks.

As Margaret applied her final touches of rouge, Jackie flounced into the room, wearing a dress in deep green that contrasted beautifully with her strawberry blonde hair and enhanced her golden-green eyes. Margaret noticed that her sister-in-law was just beginning to show that she was with child.

Jackie glanced at her friend and stuck her sultry red lip out in a frown, saying in a pout, "It is so unfair that you, chéri, after having two children, are still so small, while I am as big as a chalet."

Margaret laughed, replying in jest, "I hardly think that you are as huge as a cottage. A cow perhaps, but a cottage… never think it."

Jackie rustled over to a nearby chair and threw herself into it with the back of one hand flying to her brow—always the dramatist.

"I look so unattractive. I could almost pass for old Lady Ginine." Both women smirked at the mention of Jackie's archnemesis back in France. Continuing her tirade, she added, "Whatever will I do? You look the picture of desire, chéri. All the men will flock to you, and I, I will be left in the background trying not to drink all the champagne."

Margaret shook her head. Jackie always felt a failure unless she knew every heart would swoon in her path.

"I doubt that, my dear friend. You will, as always, break many hearts this eve."

The door opened and Cort, followed by Randall, entered Margaret's room dressed in their formal attire. Both men were wearing the traditional black and white suits, although Randall had opted for tails, a top hat with a white bowtie, and was carrying a black cane with an ivory hilt. Cort had gone the more basic route—true to his cowboy nature—and wore a simple but tailored coat with a black bowtie while choosing not to wear a hat or carry a cane.

"What is this? Are we moving the ball to my room?"

The two men looked at each other, then realized she was joking and chuckled.

"We were just coming to find if the ladies are ready to go, since we have taken care of our part and hitched up the wagon," Randall said as he took his wife's hand and placed it on his arm, ushering her out of the room.

Cort approached his wife, saying, "You look beautiful. If for nothing else, seeing you all fancied up like that makes me glad that we are going tonight."

Margaret smiled up at him. "As am I. It has been so long since I have gone somewhere or done something that truly reminds me of home."

He gently took her left hand and kissed the top of it, then placed it on his arm as he escorted her out of the room.

As they got into the wagon, Margaret realized how odd it was to be getting into a wagon in formal wear when the last time she had been dressed up like that, she went by carriage. Things were so different in America. Even after the past few years, she still was not completely used to the ways of the place.

The York castle—there was no other word to describe the house that the French-English couple had built on their land just outside Boulder—was on the opposite end of Margaret and her family's property. Margaret had not seen an estate like it since she had been back in the old country.

Lady Regina was of French noble decent and always made it a point to make it clear—yet she had no visible French accent and sported a notably English one instead. She had invited Margaret on several occasions to come calling, but Margaret had always declined, claiming that she had far too much to do at the present time and would come calling at a later date.

Jackie, on the other hand, had jumped at the chance to visit Lady Regina and gather gossip, reciting it later to Margaret only hours after each visit.

Lady Regina and Lord Gregory had also called on the Westcotts after Margaret's return and once after church to see if Margaret was sick since she had not been to church until last week. Margaret had made polite excuses but did not volunteer any more information than necessary.

Wagons littered the drive of the York estate as women in beautiful gowns and men in formal suits paraded into the entry hall where Lady Regina received her guests with her husband at her side.

When Margaret and her party finally arrived at the front, Lady Regina did not disguise a look of surprise that crossed her face as Margaret presented herself with a graceful curtsy.

"My, my, dear, it is so wonderful to see you at our gathering. We had not expected your presence. You do us a great honor."

Margaret gave a half smile, irritated that everyone assumed they knew her and what to expect of her. None of them had known her before she left Europe and how she used to love to come to balls. They had been practically the only thing she had lived for—that was until Witherton shattered her life twice and destroyed all her illusions with it. She was no longer enthralled with all the social trappings of her class, but it did not mean she did not enjoy a good dance every now and then.

"I thought it would be simply delightful to come see what could be mustered up out here in the rustics. It is so kind of you to have a ball, even though we are so far removed from a place where our social customs are practical. Fascinating is it not, how everyone gets done up—all these farmers and ranchers."

Lady Regina cocked her head to a slight angle, as if trying to decipher what Margaret meant. Then after thinking for a moment about her guest's statement, Lady Regina's pasted-on smile shifted into an insulted scowl.

Jackie quickly sidestepped Randall and interrupted, trying to smooth over the damage Margaret had inflicted to Lady Regina's pride. "Thank you so much, Lady Regina, for having such an exquisite ball for everyone. We do so appreciate what you have done."

"No, thank you, my dear Jacquelyn. You grace us so much with your presence." She glanced at the others, completely skipping over Margaret entirely, and then continued. "You and your family are most welcome here. It simply would not have been the same if the Earl of Renwick and his wife were not here."

Margaret blanched and quickly turned to face her brother. How had Lady Regina found out that Randall was the Earl of Renwick? They had left their titles behind. Had Randall, against her advisement, been giving out his title?

After one look at Randall, Margaret knew that was not the case. Randall, also jolted by the turn the conversation had taken, quickly tried to cover by saying, "I think you are mistaken, Lady Regina. I have no title." He gestured to his family, "None of us do."

Lady Regina smirked. "Oh, come now, Lord Wellesley, do not be so modest. It is quite admirable that you and your beautiful wife—what is her title?—oh yes, the Vicomtesse of Durante, wanted to make it here in the Americas without the help of your titles. But truly, I mean, what are we if we are not our title? After all, they are our heritage."

Jackie smiled with pleasure. She had confessed to Margaret on more than one occasion that she had missed being granted special treatment due to it. Of course, they all had, with the exception of Cort who had only been on the receiving end of some special treatment, in the negative persuasion, from his titled half brother.

But Margaret did not want it. Not now, not ever. She was just starting to feel secure again and this had to happen. And it naturally followed that, if Lady Regina somehow found out about Jackie's and Randall's titles, she would no doubt in time find out about Margaret's and Henry's and the scandal that she had tried to leave behind so long ago.

And if that happened, that meant it would be only a matter of time before Catherine—or worse, Witherton—found out where she and Henry were.

Margaret bit her lip, trying to repress the panic that was beginning to rise from the pit of her stomach. What was she going to do? How was she going to keep them safe? Margaret turned back to face Lady Regina, trying to stay civil while maintaining a pretense of being nonchalant. "How did you come to find out about our inconsequential titles anyhow?"

Lady Regina raised an eyebrow in surprise. "I never said anything about you having a title."

Margaret glanced away, angry at herself for making such a blunder. She gave herself two beats to regain her composure before saying, "Did someone tell you? Was someone trying to find us from the old country?"

Lady Regina replied, "I see that I have piqued your

interest, Lady Margaret—or should I say, Viscountess Rolantry?"

Margaret's eyes snapped up and focused on the older woman's. "Pardon?"

"Of course, you were the Countess of Renwick before you found your brother. He had been presumed dead in a shipwreck of some sorts, correct?"

Margaret's palms were starting to sweat, and she felt her heart pounding in her chest. She had not been this afraid since she had been tracked down in France. Even during all that time she had been with the Indians, she had held on and did not feel fear like this, knowing her son and husband were waiting for her at home. She only had to get back to them and they would all be together again. But if Catherine found her, she would take Henry away. And if Witherton found her first…. He would want vengeance for what she did to him in France. She knew Cort would not let anything happen to them without a fight. He would defend his family, even if it meant his life.

She had already lost two husbands by the hand of Witherton; she was not about to lose another man she loved by his doing. Perhaps it was time for her and Henry to run again. When it was safe—if it were ever safe again—she could come back to Cort….

Cort stepped forward, trying to deflect attention from his wife. "I think you are mistaken. My wife has no title, and I think I would know."

Lady Regina, recognizing that she should not challenge

a man, especially in the West, graciously nodded. "Perhaps I was mistaken."

Margaret put her shaking hand on Cort's arm, trying to steady herself so as not to faint and cause a scene.

Still needing to know how she knew, Margaret asked one last time, forcing her voice not to quiver. "Who happened to mention all this information about us to you, Lady Regina? If it is someone from our past—an old friend or some such—we would like to get reacquainted with them if they are still in town."

Lady Regina shrugged, replying, "I am sure that if they want to be found, they will be." Glancing past them to the next guests in line, she added in a dismissive tone, "If you will excuse me, my husband and I need to greet the rest of our guests before dinnertime."

The two couples moved through the entry hall and into the parlor where most of the other assembled guests were already mingling.

Cort looked down at Margaret and seemed to be measuring what to do. He remained silent. Randall, on the other hand, always began to ramble when the pressure was on. "Maggie, what can I do to help you? Do you need a glass of punch, something to nibble on? Mayhap you want me to guide you over to a seat?"

Margaret looked over to her brother and shook her head, saying in a mere whisper, "Nothing, thank you."

Randall shot a look to Cort, as if asking, 'What should we do now?'

Cort gently rubbed his wife's hand. "Margaret, I promise you, it will be all right."

She blinked back the tears that were painfully pushing from behind her eyes as she distractedly brushed a loose curl from out of her face. When she looked up at her husband, she could tell from the look in his eyes that he really believed what he said. But Witherton would not stop until he found them—until he had taken back what he believed was rightfully his to possess.

"Do you want to go home? I can make excuses to the Yorks for us."

Margaret shook her head. "No, that would only cause more suspicion by the Yorks, and I do not want that. As is, all my questions probably did enough damage to do us all in."

Cort shook his head. "I hardly think that Lady Regina or Lord Gregory can do much harm with knowing that you three are titled."

"Then *you* do not know much of anything." Margaret regretted saying it the moment the snide comment slipped out of her mouth. The look of hurt that Cort tried to conceal was almost her undoing.

Trying to rectify her blunder, she blurted out, "I am so sorry, Cort. I did not mean that. It is just… I am so scared of who told her and who else they told and who the Yorks might tell. If Cath—" Margaret lowered her voice so that no one around them could hear, finishing with, "If

Catherine or Witherton find out where we are, I could lose everything I hold dear."

Cort, not wanting to draw attention to them either, said in a steely voice, "As long as I have breath, I promise you will never have to worry about losing anything you love."

Margaret licked her lips, trying to compose her racing emotions. "I hope you can keep that promise, for all our sakes."

"We should make our way toward the dining hall for dinner," Randall said. "It seems everyone is headed in that direction."

CHAPTER 24

The assembled guests were so many, two enormous tables had been set up in separate rooms.

Margaret did not know more than two people around her—other than her family—since she just recently started feeling comfortable enough to go into town. Randall, Jackie, and even Cort, however, seemed to know just about everyone present and were immersed in conversations.

Margaret sat and sipped her glass of punch daintily, paying little attention to what was going on around her. They had gone through the ten-course meal without Margaret tasting any of it. She ate out of duty, decorum, and so as not to cause any undue attention, but utterly detested every moment of it.

Finally, after what seemed like forever, the dinner part of

the evening was over and Margaret breathed a sigh of relief. At least during dancing, she did not have to converse in depth or listen to useless banter. All she had to do was dance gracefully and reply on occasion to a comment fed to her.

As Margaret and Cort approached the ballroom, for some reason—perhaps because of the thoughts of Witherton—Margaret was taken back to the time of her first ball. She had been young then, full of the naivety that comes with being merely a child, and she had been in love with the idea of love. She was no longer that little girl, and somewhere along the way, she had lost her ability to find wonder in all the little things. She missed that.

Cort smiled down at her as the music for a waltz began. "Are you ready to go out there and show them your perfect footwork?"

Margaret crinkled her nose. "I have to give you fair warning, I have not danced since I have been in the Americas."

Cort shrugged. "Then we are about even in that respect, since I have not danced since I was in the military."

With that, he pulled her out onto the ballroom floor and masterfully drew her into his arms.

It took several moments of slight stumbling before Margaret fell into step with the beat of the music. By that time, Cort already had the steps down pat.

"It seems you misled me, dear husband. You seem to be quite the expert dancer."

He chuckled. "I did have my fair share of satisfied partners in my day. Perhaps I will do the same with some tonight."

Margaret grumbled under her breath and narrowed her eyes in jealousy, not liking the idea of her husband with other women in any way, shape, or form.

"What is it, sweetheart? You seem to be a bit perturbed."

"You know full well I want to be the only partner you care to satisfy."

He winked at her. "You need not worry about that, Margaret. You are the only woman I will ever worry about pleasing for the rest of my life."

Margaret smiled up at her husband. "I am glad that we stayed, Cort. I feel better now that we are dancing. It has always made things easier for me."

"I, on the other hand, am beginning to wish we had left."

Margaret looked up with rounded eyes, surprised at Cort's sudden outburst. "Whatever for?"

"Because, my beautiful wife, I think you are far too attractive for your own good. All the men are staring at you, and I am starting to get covetous."

Margaret laughed softly. "They can look all they want, but just remember, I am going home with you tonight." She glanced around and confirmed her own suspicions. "Besides, I am not the only one who seems to be drawing attention. Look at all *your* adoring fans."

And indeed, Cort had been growing a following. Young

women all around the room were staring at him. Margaret was not surprised one bit. Her husband was very easy on the eyes.

"Suddenly it seems we are the most popular people around," Cort stated with incredulity.

Margaret laughed full force that time, and a few heads turned to see what could make the beauty in blue laugh so loud.

"Hush now or you might make a scene," Cort teased.

Margaret rolled her eyes. "As if I care one little bit. These people are so fickle. They might like us right now, but tomorrow, we will be old news. They only watch us now because we have never come to anything before."

Just as Cort was about to retort, the music ended. Margaret curtsied and Cort bowed slightly, both of them feeling awkward since they had never been formal with each other since the day they met. When someone saved your life, it negated the need to keep things formal afterward.

Cort escorted his wife off the dance floor, and as soon as they exited, a swarm of young gentlemen and ladies bombarded them. Swiftly, each of them were being pulled onto the floor to dance with someone else.

Cort gave Margaret one last look of masked annoyance over his shoulder as a voluptuous blonde in red climbed into his arms for the next dance.

Margaret had managed to escape into the arms of her brother, who laughed lightly as he guided his twin onto the floor.

"You look as if you could throttle that highly attractive blonde who has herself wrapped nicely in your husband's arms."

Margaret blasted a dirty look up at Randall. "I will thank you kindly not to make this any worse."

"Cheer up, old mum. It is not all that bad. He might not even notice her…." Randall's voice trailed off as they both glanced over when Cort laughed lightly as the girl said something with a smile.

"You were saying."

"I think the only way to win this battle and prove that you are just as desirable is to not avoid the next gentleman who wants to dance with you. Fight fire with fire, Mags. Believe me, you have plenty of it."

She grinned up at her brother. "All right, Rand, if that is what you think I should do. I cannot argue with elders, now can I?"

Randall snickered. "Elder by three minutes, as you pointed out in our last disagreement."

The song ended, and Randall escorted his sister off and patted her on the back, saying in a barely audible whisper, "Go fight the fire, Maggie."

Margaret tried to muster up the strength to make eye contact with one of the gentlemen standing around her while letting down her guard that kept them at bay. Just as she was about to give up hope, Margaret heard a voice from behind her say, "You look as beautiful as ever, Lady Margaret, even after all these years."

Margaret whirled around and her mouth fell open in a gasp. "Pierre, is that truly you?"

The years had been kind to Pierre, her childhood friend and confidant from France. He looked as handsome as he ever did, with his slicked black hair and dark eyes contrasting against his pale skin. He wore his tailored black suit exceptionally well, and flashes of feelings came flooding back to Margaret.

He smiled sheepishly. "I daresay, I was not sure you would greet me with much enthusiasm."

She pursed her lips in hurt. "Pierre, you were my dearest friend for the first year right after Henry's death. You stood by me, gave both my infant son and me a place to live. By all the stars, of course I am happy to see you."

Forgetting for a moment where she was, Margaret rushed up and threw her arms around him. At first, Pierre stood still, shocked by Margaret's sudden outburst of affection—so uncharacteristic of her nature. Then he embraced her back for several seconds before kissing her lightly on the forehead.

Gasps were heard around the room as people watched the truly beautiful couple, with dark good looks and smoldering gazes, exchange a forbidden embrace in front of nearly the entire population of Boulder.

Randall caught the exchange as well as he danced with his wife.

"Well, I did tell her to fight fire with fire. But I did not mean burn the whole place down in the process," Randall said as he glanced over at Cort, who also had seen the situation and was currently trying to disentangle himself from his most recent admirer. "This does not look to be good, Jackie dear. I think I need to get my sister under control while you do the same for your cousin."

For the first time, Jackie looked past her husband to see the predicament that Margaret had gotten herself into.

Jackie stopped midstep and put her hands over her mouth, exclaiming, "Oh, Randy, why did you not say something sooner that my cousin, Pierre, was here." With that, Jackie picked up her skirts and rushed, as much as a pregnant woman could, over to where her best friend and cousin stood.

Randall stood for a moment, adjusting to what just transpired. A few people looked at him and he nodded awkwardly to each one while trying to maintain a look of ease as he made his way over to where his wife had just stopped.

"Pierre, cousin dear, I can hardly believe that it is you. We both have missed you deeply," Jackie said as she placed a peck upon his cheek.

"Yes, well, if you perhaps had left a forwarding place of lodging, I could have visited. As it happens, my friend Lord William Almonbury, the son of the Viscount Braybridge, was coming over to the Americas to check on some business holdings he purchased in the Oregon Territory and asked me to come along. It turns out, his friend Louis was coming to live with his grandparents here in Boulder, and he asked both of us to come along before we headed to Oregon. I had my investigator, Mulchere, look into your whereabouts and he had tracked down your boarding information to America, but his contacts lost track of you after you arrived in New York." He looked around and said quietly, "Perhaps we should finish this conversation on the veranda where there are fewer ears, if you know what I mean."

Both women nodded and then followed a few feet behind his retreating figure.

Once outside, Pierre turned back around and continued where he had left off. "I had hoped, as I traveled here in the West, that I might be able to look into some loose leads he had, but it was only when Lady Regina mentioned a woman whom she believed to be of French nobility by the name of Jacquelyn that I had a suspicion it might be my dear cousin who disappeared on me. Come to find out that she mentioned an English woman named Margaret who had a son named Henry. Once that piece was added, the puzzle started coming together very quickly. I knew something had happened bad enough to make you all disappear without a trace."

Both women looked at each other, then back to Pierre. Margaret asked defensively, "Does anyone else know we are here?"

He shook his head. "Not that I am aware of, but Lady Regina has many friends back in the old country, and I am sure this will make interesting news to write to them about." Then, almost as if he could not hold it in any longer, Pierre blurted out, addressing the question to both ladies, "Why didn't you tell me where you were going? Leave some sort of clue so I could find you?"

Margaret shifted her gaze away from him. Jackie grimaced, then finally replied, "Because if you could unravel the clue, so could anyone else who found it."

"But you both know me. I would never let anyone find out where you were."

"Truly? Then tell me, how did *he* find out about me from some French admirer who was talking about me in an English pub?"

Pierre looked stricken. "What are you implying?"

"I am stating that you got drunk one night while you were nursing your wounds and shot off your mouth about me. His spies picked up on it and tracked me down in France. H*e* came after me and attacked me again." Then, with a shudder, she added in a whisper, "And *he* threatened to tell Catherine were I was so she could take my son."

Pierre furrowed his brows together in confusion. "But I never went to any pubs during my visit to England while you were in France. I was far too busy with my business. I did, however, run into Eduard Voclain in England, and I would not be surprised if he frequented a few pubs while he was painting over there."

Margaret grew pale with the realization that all this time she had blamed Pierre, when it had been a man from a chance encounter at a dinner party in France who had caused the series of events that led up to Michel's death. She had a bad habit of jumping to the wrong conclusions about people. She needed to ask God to help her stop from doing it anymore.

"I am so sorry, Pierre. I had thought that you.... I have no excuse." She reached out and placed her hand on his arm. "Please, please forgive me."

"How could I ever not grant you anything, Margaret? You know I would do anything for you."

Margaret smiled at him and leaned up, giving him a kiss on the cheek, but before she knew what was happening, he had turned his mouth to catch hers.

Margaret's eyes popped open in shock. What was he doing?

And as bad luck would have it, Cort chose that precise moment to walk out and find the three of them nestled behind a few trees.

"What do you think you are doing, kissing my wife?"

Pierre jerked back sharply, abashed for kissing another man's wife. Margaret, not wanting Pierre and Cort to get in a fight, and knowing Pierre meant nothing by it, said quickly in his defense, "It meant nothing, Cort. We are old friends."

Cort stiffened, balling up his fists at his side. Margaret became apprehensive when she saw that all-too-familiar mixture of savage-cowboy justice gleaming in his eyes. He was getting ready to fight like the first day she met him. Pierre did not stand a chance.

Margaret stepped in front of Pierre, holding out her hand. "He took me in when I had nowhere else to go. He protected Henry and me simply because he cared about us. You cannot do this, Cort. I know this seems like a compromising situation, but Jackie will back me on this. Nothing was meant by what you saw. Pierre is like a brother to me."

Cort unclenched his fists and, unnoticeably to everyone besides Margaret, willed himself to relax.

Pierre, ever the gentleman, stepped forward, bowed, and stuck out his hand. "My name is Pierre Girard, the Vidame of Demoulin, cousin to Lady Jacquelyn Seandra Allantes, Vicomtesse of Durante."

Jackie automatically corrected, "Jacquelyn Learingam, Countess of Renwick now."

Pierre shot his cousin a look of surprise. "You married Margaret's brother, Randall?"

"They eloped right before we left France." Margaret moved toward her husband and put her hand in the crook of his arm. "This is my husband, Cortland Westcott."

It was then that Cort finally took Pierre's extended hand, gripping tight and shaking firmly. "Everyone calls me Cort."

"Then by all means, you must call me Pierre."

Just as the two men let go of each other's hand, Randall exploded on the scene, the frustration from getting lost in the garden showing on his face.

"There you all are. I had wondered where you had all gotten off to. Pierre, it is good to see you again." He looked between the two men and sighed. "Glad to see it did not come to blows."

Cort, still uneasy and full of irritation, shifted his weight and then looked down at his wife. "Are you ready to come back in?"

Margaret peeked over at Pierre and saw a look on his face that worried her. He seemed desperate to talk to her privately. But as she glanced up at her husband, she saw that it would not go over well if she decided to stay out there alone with him.

"We all should go in, and after I dance the next song with my husband, I will take a turn with you, Pierre," she said, raising her eyebrows enough for Pierre, Jackie, and Randall to notice.

Jackie put her hand on her cousin's arm and asked, "You will dance with me when we get inside, won't you, cousin?"

Dutifully, Pierre nodded, yet maintained his gaze on Margaret while saying, "I would be honored."

The five members—tied together in several bizarre twists of fate—made their way into the ballroom.

CHAPTER 25

Once inside, without saying another word, Cort swirled his wife onto the dance floor and masterfully began to lead her in another waltz.

After several moments of awkward silence, Cort finally spoke up. "How many more surprising secrets plan to pop up from your past?"

Margaret pressed her lips together tightly, recognizing her husband's veiled anger. "He was not a secret, Cort. There was just never a need for me to mention Pierre to you. I left that part of my life behind long ago, and it seemed so inconsequential. I had no idea that anything that took place during that time would bear weight on our future. As it turns out, Pierre's being here is mere coincidence. But to be honest, it is nice to see him since he is one of my oldest friends and we did not part on such good terms the last time I saw him."

"I wish you had told me about him. This incident makes me wonder how many more men you have in your past."

"What are you implying?"

"I see the way he looks at you. He was in love with you back in France, and if I am not mistaken, he is still in love with you. How many other broken hearts did you leave behind in your wake of escape?"

Margaret stiffened, feeling attacked for the first time ever by Cort.

"Not many, I assure you. And as for Pierre, at every opportunity, I tried to dissuade him from pursuing me. He just never gave up."

"It seems he still has not." Cort nodded toward where Pierre was dancing with Jackie but watching them with unwavering persistence.

"If he is as you say, I am sure he will soon see that I am completely in love with my husband and nothing or anyone is going to change that."

Margaret felt Cort's demeanor unwind slightly as he said, "I know that, but it is good to hear it, especially considering the circumstances."

"I mean it. I do, you know. I love you, with all my heart."

After this last statement, Margaret saw Cort visibly loosen up as he smiled down at her. "All right, I will let all of this go, but I don't want to catch you kissing another man as long as I live."

Margaret laughed with relief. "No doubt, if I did, you would lock me up in the cellar and never let me out."

Cort winked, then teased, "Of course I would let you out, but only to kiss me."

Margaret playfully smacked him on the side of the arm with her gloved hand. As they continued to dance, she said lightheartedly, "Oh, you. Quit joshing me."

The couple continued to dance until the waltz ended. Cort escorted his wife off the dance floor and over to where Lord and Lady York stood.

"How do you do, Lord York, Lady York," Margaret said, curtsying with ease as Cort gave a small bow. "It is good to see you both again."

"We are doing quite well. Thank you, Mister and Missus Westcott, for asking," Lady York said with a firm smile.

Margaret felt someone tap her on the shoulder, then heard Pierre's familiar voice ask, "May I have the honor of this dance, Margaret? I do believe you promised it to me while we were outside on the veranda."

Margaret turned to faced Pierre, replying, "Why yes, Pierre, you may have this dance." Then she paused while looking up and over her shoulder at her husband, adding, "Of course, as long as my husband consents."

Cort bobbed his head, eyeing Pierre carefully as he said each word, "I have no objection with two childhood friends dancing for old time's sake."

Pierre nodded. "How good of you, sir. I am much obliged and consider it an honor to be able to share a dance with a woman"—he looked down at Margaret—"as splendid as your wife."

Lady Regina interjected. "Why, Pierre, it is so good to see that you have finally met up with Lady Margaret." She paused, then added with a taunt to Margaret, "Or should I now call you Viscountess Rolantry?"

"Missus Westcott will do just fine, thank you," Margaret said with a thin voice.

With that, Margaret put her hand in the crook of Pierre's arm and pressed lightly with her fingertips, signaling him to lead her onto the dance floor.

Gracefully, Pierre gathered Margaret up for the next dance as he said, "It feels good to have you back in my arms." He looked deep into her violet eyes. "It has been a long time."

Averting her attention from his penetrating gaze, Margaret replied, "Yes, it has."

"When I left France, you were engaged to the marquis. I heard he had died quite mysteriously and you, along with my cousin and your brother, disappeared without so much as a word. Now I find you married to another man here in the Americas. It seems that a time for you and me to be together never quite seems to fit into the cards. Tell me, what does this Yank cowboy have that I do not?"

Margaret finally met Pierre's eyes and stated with certainty, "My heart."

His feet faltered slightly, something she had never known Pierre to do, and she realized that Cort's suspicion was most correct. Pierre was indeed still in love with her.

"I suppose that means my plan to sweep you off your feet and entice you to run away with me would come to no avail?"

"Quite."

"Then it seems that I will have to settle for being only friends—a hard thing for a Frenchman to settle for, especially losing one's object of attention to an *American*."

Margaret laughed lightly. "You forget, Pierre, I too am now an American."

He raised an eyebrow in question. "I hardly think that you could ever be considered part of these people." He gestured to the surrounding guests. "After all, you are a European, a woman of the continent, and English at that. Do your people not take the most pride in your heritage?"

"It is true, but since I have made my home here with Cort, this place has become my heritage. I had to leave everything behind when I fled Europe. But oddly enough, I find myself more in love with America than I ever did with England or France." She smiled as she thought of her husband. "Love tends to make everything seem so much better."

Pierre grimly smiled back. "You really do love him. I can see that now."

Margaret nodded. "He is the best thing that has ever happened to me."

"I am surprised to hear you say that, considering your first husband and the marquis."

"Cort treats me as an equal, and he not only allows me but wants me to be my own person. That means a great deal to me."

"Then I am glad for you. You deserve to be happy, Margaret. And if *he* does that, then I will make it my best attempt to get along with him."

"Thank you, Pierre. I want the two of you to be friends. I think that, given the chance, both of you would find that you are a lot alike."

"Perhaps. We shall see."

"By the by, how long do you plan to stay with Lord and Lady York?"

"Until week's end."

"You are leaving that soon?"

"Yes, well, it seems that the business Lord Almonbury need to take care of in the Oregon Territory is more pressing than he first ascertained. But I will be back through in a few months and we can spend a great deal more time together then."

"I am glad to hear that. It is good to see you, Pierre. I have missed you tremendously."

"I feel the same. I did not truly know how much I missed you until I saw you again tonight."

The song ended and Pierre escorted Margaret back over to Cort, who was standing with Randall and Jackie.

"I have brought back your wife safe and sound, sir."

"Thank you, I appreciate it."

Jackie moved quickly over to Pierre's side, saying, "It is my turn now to dance with you, dear cousin. We have a great deal of catching up to do, do we not?"

He nodded and allowed Jackie to pull him onto the dance floor for the song that had just started.

Cort looked over at his wife, then said, "This turned out to be a far more interesting night than I had expected."

"Indeed."

"Are you ready to take your leave?"

Margaret nodded. "I am feeling quite tired, it seems."

"Then let us go home."

The ball had gone way into the wee morning hours—at least that was what Jackie had told Margaret the day after.

Several days had passed without disturbance.

It was jam season, and Margaret was canning as much fruit as she could before any could spoil. She had to admit, she was actually quite good at it. Out of all her chores, she excelled at it the most.

As she placed one of the last jars of strawberries in the pantry, she heard a rap at the front door. Making her way through the house, Margaret patted down her hair that had gone wild as she did her work.

On the other side of the door stood Pierre. Surprised at the unscheduled visit, Margaret invited him inside. "What a surprise, Pierre. If I knew you were coming, I would have cleaned up a bit."

Pierre glanced down at her attire for the first time and reacted with surprise. "It seems the Americas have domesticated you, my noble Margaret. I never would have pictured you as the hired help."

"I am not hired help, Pierre. I am the ranch owner's wife. There is a big difference."

"From the looks of it," he said, gesturing to her stained apron, "the two do not seem so far apart."

Margaret blushed at the way she must look. Noticing that he had embarrassed her, Pierre quickly added, "I am sorry, Margaret. I did not mean to offend you."

She avoided a reply and stated instead, "I was just making some tea for the afternoon break. Would you care to stay on for some?"

Pierre paused for a moment and then shook his head. "Even though that sounds very tempting, and I would love to spend some time with you alone, I need to say what I came to say and then be on my way."

Margaret frowned, noticing the all-too-serious tone in Pierre's voice. "What is it?"

"Let us sit down, Margaret."

They made their way into the living room where Margaret and Pierre sat on the western-styled sofa in the center of the room.

"All right, we are sitting. What is it that you want to tell me?"

"Margaret, you know that your interests are always the utmost of my concern?"

"Yes."

"Then, when I tell you this, do not think of it as a jealous ex-beau telling you. Think objectively and take it quite serious."

"I will."

"Good, I feel I can continue, then. The other morning, I had an uneasy feeling about your husband. So I made some inquiries, checked into some information, and I found out some rather disturbing news."

Stiffening, Margaret placed her clasped hands in her lap. "What is it?"

"Margaret, Cort is not who he says he is. Actually, I found out something very alarming about him."

"Pierre, just come out with it."

"I do not want to be the one to tell you. I want him to be the one. Ask him about his half brother. It is very important that he tell you who he is and their connection."

"But he has already told me about him and what happened between them."

"Yes, that is possible, but I am certain he did not tell you everything. I know for a fact that there is one very important piece of information that he has left out. I do not think you would have married him if you had known."

Margaret narrowed her eyes, thinking this was a ploy of Pierre's to put a wedge between her and Cort. "Pierre, nothing can come between Cort and me."

"I would not be so sure of that if I were you. What he withheld will change everything. I am only telling you this because I love you, Margaret, and feel you need to know the truth."

"I love you too. I appreciate you looking out for me, but I am sure it is nothing to fret about, Pierre. When the time is right, I will ask my husband about his half brother."

"Well, I did what I came for and delivered the message. I hope you take it to heart."

"I will."

Pierre leaned over to hug Margaret and kiss her on the cheek. "I will see you soon when I come back through on my way back to France."

"I look forward to it."

"As do I."

CHAPTER 26

Several weeks had passed since Pierre told her there was a secret Cort was keeping from her, one that would change the dynamic of their relationship forever. Margaret tried to convince herself that whatever Pierre had found out about Cort did not matter, but part of her feared what it might be. She had fallen for men with secrets in the past, and she thought she and Cort had divulged everything between them before they were married. What was he keeping from her, and why? She knew she needed to discuss the matter with her husband before it could create division between them.

Margaret made her way out to the corral where Cort was working with a new colt. She watched her husband for several moments, taking in his good looks. She never got tired of watching him work with their horses. He moved in such a hypnotic way as he guided them around the corral and through their workouts.

"Cort, I have something I need to discuss with you."

Margaret patted Chester's back and released him to go over to the feeding trough.

Cort leaned his arms across the corral top as he placed one of his booted feet on the bottom rail. "What is it, sweetheart?"

"I told you Pierre came by before he left to make his way to the Oregon territory."

"Yes, you mentioned he came to say goodbye."

"He did not come just to say goodbye. He also came to tell me something he felt I should know. I had been debating whether or not I should bring it up to you, but he told me there is something in your past you have purposely kept from me."

Cort stiffened as he furrowed his eyebrows together. "What did he say?"

"He said I needed to ask you about your half brother."

"I had wanted to tell you from the moment I realized the truth."

"What is the truth, Cort? What have you been keeping from me?"

Cort took in a deep breath and squared his shoulders. "I should have told you this a long time ago. I wanted to, but I was afraid. There is history between the Duke of Witherton and me."

Still not understanding what Cort was trying to say, she asked, "What do you mean?"

Cort paused for a long moment, then said in a small, still tone, "I am his half brother. He was the reason I had to leave Europe and hide in America."

Margaret pulled away from his grasp and stepped back, staring at her husband in shock. Moments flickered by without a word between them. Finally, Cort said, "Say something. Anything."

Margaret turned her head to the side, averting her gaze. "You knew all this time and said nothing?"

"Yes."

She looked back at Cort with hurt gleaming deep within her eyes. "Why?" she asked with a betrayed voice.

"I thought I was protecting you."

"No. No, you were protecting yourself. You thought, if I knew, I would not marry you."

"Would you have married me?"

"You robbed me of the chance to make that decision. We will never know now."

Without another word, Margaret turned and ran toward the house.

Margaret was on the back porch washing the laundry in an enormous tub. The excessive heat made the chore more difficult. But what made the work seem even more demanding that day was being unable to focus solely on it, causing the work to take even longer. Her mind continued to dwell on the secret that Cort had revealed to her the previous day. Somehow, it changed everything, but in a way she would have never expected.

As she reflected on the situation and their connection, it was the vast differences between Cort and Witherton that stuck out. Cort embodied everything that was good and right, and even the reason he did not tell her about his connection to Witherton seemed to be motivated out of a place of love and protection. She had said in hurt and anger that he only did it to protect himself, but she knew the man she was married to, and he was never motivated by selfish reasons. Everything Cort did was for the people he loved, which was the exact opposite of Witherton. Every decision that Witherton ever made was for his own selfish design; nothing mattered but what he wanted.

But what made the difference between them?

By all rights, Cort had every reason to be bitter and angry over the things that had been done to him and the hand he had been dealt. Instead, he pursued righteousness and love above all else.

And then there was Witherton, who had been given every privilege and advantage possible, but nothing was ever enough and nothing was sacred. Instead, he would leave a wake of destruction in his path with no regard to whom he hurt.

The difference between them was obvious. The words

her father had quoted to her from the Bible, all those years prior, came floating back. *"Love is gracious and honest. It can withstand anything and always bears hope.... You see, love is not only a feeling but an action. Even when your heart does not feel like loving, you act it out. Emotions are fickle, and one moment you feel one way, and the next you feel completely different. But true love will act and trust that the heart will follow behind."*

Through God, Cort personified the very essence of true love. All this time, she had been fighting against giving up control to God, but it was the very thing that made Cort the man she loved. How could she have been so blind all this time? She could never be the wife Cort deserved, the mother her children needed, or the friend her family merited because she was incapable of perfect love without letting God manifest it through her.

Margaret whispered softly, "God, I have made so many mistakes in my life. I did not listen to my father when I was young, I did not trust Henry when he was alive, and I have hurt Cort more times than I can count. God, I need you, and I am so sorry for not trusting in you completely. Help me. Help me be the woman, the wife, the mother, the friend you want me to be. I give myself to you, every part of me, even the parts no one else knows or sees."

By the end of the prayer, Margaret was crying gently, though they were not tears of sadness but of pure joy. She needed to find Cort and tell him she forgave him.

She found him cleaning out one of the stalls and had a twinge of pride as she saw how hard he worked to further their dreams. Nothing was beneath him, not even cleaning out horse dung.

"Cort, I have had time to think about our last conversation. I have come to a decision on the matter."

He stopped what he was doing and turned to look at her. He placed the bottom of the shovel on the ground and leaned on it.

A fearful look cross his face as he asked, "Have you come to tell me you are leaving me?"

Margaret balked at his question. "On the contrary, I have come to tell you I forgive you for keeping the secret from me and I understand why you did it."

Cort let out a sigh of relief. "I am glad to hear that, Margaret. The way you left things, you had me worried."

"You have forgiven me so much and have loved me through even more. I refuse to let Witherton take one more thing from me."

"Do you not worry about our shared connection? That we are cut from the same cloth?"

"I know, without a shadow of a doubt, that you are nothing like that despicable man. You are honest, trustworthy, faithful, and selfless. You are a wonderful husband and father and the love of my life."

Tears formed in the corner of Cort's eyes. "Margaret, you have no idea how much it means to hear you say that. I knew from the moment I saw you that you were the love of mine as well."

He dropped the shovel and pulled her to him. Leaning

down, he kissed her with a passion that took Margaret's breath away. She could feel in his kiss that he wanted her to know nothing would ever tear them apart.

CHAPTER 27

While checking her pantry for the ingredients needed to bake the week's worth of bread, Margaret realized she needed to go to the market to purchase several of the items.

"I have to go into town today, Cort, to pick up some supplies. I want to bake some scones and we do not have enough flour or sugar."

"Do you want me to come with you?" he asked, momentarily looking up from the lead he was handling.

"No, but I think I will take Henry in with me. I think he would enjoy playing the man of the house at the store. Do you mind taking a break in about a half hour so you can keep an eye on Susan. She's napping currently, but should wake up by then."

Cort nodded as he walked over closer. "All right, be safe

and make sure to get back before nightfall." He kissed her lightly on the lips, then almost as an afterthought, he added, "And be sure to take a gun with you. I heard someone thought they spotted Indians up on the ridge. It's probably nothing, but you can never be too careful."

Margaret smiled. "I love the way you are so overprotective."

"I have had to learn the lesson the hard way. I do not need to learn it again. I will see you when you get home."

Nodding, Margaret turned around and headed toward the barn, calling out behind her, "Henry, darling, I am going into town. Do you wish to come?"

Scampering feet were heard from around the corral as a voice said, "Wait for me, Mother."

Expecting her to be already at the barn, Henry slammed into the back of Margaret.

"Anxious to get to town, are we?"

Henry stepped back quickly, nodding. "Yes, Tommy Neilson told me at school on Friday he was going to show me his new pet frog the next time I was in town. He just got it, but he isn't allowed to bring it to school anymore on account it jumped right onto Miss Tucker. Tommy says that Hopper—his frog—can jump over six feet in the air."

Margaret laughed. "And I am quite sure that Tommy will no doubt need to show you this in detail. Good thing we are going into town." Then, remembering what Cort had mentioned, Margaret told Henry, "Go inside the house and get one of the handguns and one of the rifles while I hitch up the wagon."

She liked to be prepared, and one gun, when it came to confrontations, never seemed to be enough.

"All right, Mother."

Margaret watched as her son ran toward the house, then slipped through the door. Afterward, she turned back around and continued over to the barn.

Just as Margaret was finishing hitching up one of the previous year's foals to the wagon, Henry met with her, the in hand. Together, they lead the colt and wagon out of the barn.

"Why are we taking so many guns, Mother?"

"It is always important to have plenty of protection. Remember: it is always better to be overprepared than under."

Henry nodded. "I will remember that, Mother."

"Good, then let us head into town." Margaret grabbed the edge of the wagon seat and climbed up into the passenger seat.

As Henry hopped driver's side, Margaret said, "When we arrive in town, make sure to wait for me. I do not want you running off to Tommy's like a wild child."

Henry chuckled as he took the reigns in hand. "Yes, Mother. We would not want to be the town spectacle."

Margaret blinked several times without saying a word. That was the first time that Henry had ever said anything remotely adult-like. She had not been prepared for his quick-witted sarcasm or the very manly laugh that ushered in his sudden appearance of becoming a man. She was beginning to realize that, not only was her son starting to look like a young man, but his mind was also rapidly following behind.

After several minutes of driving in silence, Henry asked, "What's the matter, Mother? You seem perturbed."

"My, my, we are using big words these days."

"All my schoolwork has really paid off, I suppose. I feel like I have a real knack for it."

"What do you mean?"

Henry paused a moment while he switched the reins into his other hand, then glanced back behind him and pulled out a book. He handed it over to his mother.

Margaret scanned the cover of the book: Lord Byron's *Don Juan*. "This is highly unusual reading for a boy in his second year of school."

"I am not reading it for school."

"Then why are you reading it? And where did you get it?"

"I am reading it for a challenging pleasure, as Miss Tucker would say, and I got it from Mister Davendale. When I told Miss Tucker that I wanted something more demanding to read, she told me to go see Mister Davendale because he had an extensive private library that might have something that would suit me."

"Is this the first book you have borrowed from him?"

"No, there have been a few before."

"How many?" Margaret asked before holding a waterskin up to her lips and taking a drink.

"Umm… I think somewhere around twenty."

Margaret choked, letting a few drops of water dribble out of her mouth. Embarrassed at her lack of manners, she held her hand up to her mouth and dabbed the water away.

"That many? You have read twenty books of this caliber?"

Henry shrugged. "Some I just skimmed. But here's the best part. When I read, I can instantly recall anything from that book."

Margaret's mouth gaped open as she blurted out, "Henry, how is that possible? How much of this book do you have memorized?"

"All of it."

"All of it? How can that be?" she asked in astonishment.

"I don't really know. I've found that whenever I look at anything, I can remember it effortlessly. The same happens with any word. If I don't know what it means, I look it up, and then it sticks in my mind."

"This is simply amazing, Henry. I can hardly believe what I am hearing. I think you have a gift." She reached over and squeezed her son's arm. "You could become anything you wanted, Henry—a doctor, a lawyer, a magistrate."

"They are called senators here, Mother."

"Oh, I knew that. I only forgot. But don't you see? The possibilities are endless. What I would not have given to be able to have the opportunities that you are going to have when you finish school."

Henry frowned, then asked after a few moments, "You were not happy with my real father, were you?"

Margaret's head snapped to the side. "Of course I was happy with your father. I loved him. I still love him very much."

"Then why do you sound as if you regret the decisions of your past?"

He was getting too perceptive these days. It was getting harder to avoid talking about their past and all the circumstances that surrounded their forced departure to America.

"Listen to me very carefully about this, Henry. I do not regret marrying your father. He made me happier than I had ever thought possible. Your father and you are two of the very best things that ever happened to me, and I am thankful every day that Henry gave me you before he left this world. Do not *ever* doubt that."

Henry nodded. "So, what do you think I should study for? The schoolwork I am doing now is terribly easy, and I have all this free time on my hands."

"I think I will talk with Miss Tucker and see if we can get you on an advanced course of study. If you get done rapidly, you can go to university even earlier than we had expected."

"I would like that, Mother. I have this deep desire to learn. I feel as if the more I learn, the more power I gain."

He laughed for a few seconds and then added, "I have no idea from where this deep-burning desire comes."

"I think your gift gives you that desire. But remember, temperance is the key to maintaining power."

Henry nodded as they pulled into the outskirts of town.

Margaret looked over at her son and forced herself to remember that he was only seven years old, despite the lengthy intellectual discussion they had just shared.

"You astound me, darling."

Henry smiled over at her. "Thank you, Mother."

CHAPTER 28

After pulling the wagon to a halt outside the town grocery, Henry hopped down from the wagon and made his way around to Margaret's side, then reached up to help his mother down.

As soon as his mother was safely free of the wagon, Henry begged, "Can I go see Tommy's frog now?" And as quickly as the young man appeared, the little boy took back over.

"Yes, of course you can. But make sure you are back here in twenty minutes. You need to help me load the wagon, and if you arrive on time, I will buy you a penny candy."

"All right, mother."

And with that, he turned around and ran across the

street as Margaret yelled after him, "Twenty minutes, Henry."

Margaret made her way to the store and headed inside. The shop owner, Missus Plumes, greeted her in her thick Irish brogue. "Hello, Missus Westcott."

Margaret bowed her head slightly as she took off her bonnet. "How do you do, Missus Plumes."

"Quite well, although Mister Plumes has taken ill with a spring cold and I'm runnin' the store by myself. But Doctor Dixon says that he should be better by the end of this week, God willing."

"Then I hope to see him next time I am in. Give him my regards."

"Most certainly, Missus Westcott. And how are you doing today?"

"Oh, I am doing fairly well. Although, it has been getting harder to get my chores done with this heat spell we are having. Thank goodness I have Cort and Henry to help me."

"Yes, they're both such good ones, those two. I daresay your boy has been springing up like a weed. I scarcely recognize him when he comes in these days. And having such blond hair and that penetrating stare with those brown eyes, why he's just going to be such a little heartbreaker when he starts thinking about girls."

A pang of sadness made Margaret inwardly flinch. She wished Henry could have seen his son grow up. He was the spitting image of his father, down to the Rolantry family eyes, and it would have been something to see them next to each other.

Changing the subject, Margaret said, "I was thinking, Missus Plumes, that I would like to make some new curtains for the kitchen. The ones we have in there now are so drab. What is the newest light-colored fabric you have in stock?"

"Well, I just got this sunflower yellow in and I think you might like it. Hold on, let me go and fetch it. You wait right there."

Margaret nodded and began to study the different patterns on the table in front of her. She was still getting down the finer points of sewing and depended a great deal on detailed patterns.

Margaret stiffened as the tiny hairs on the back of her neck stood on end. She felt a presence she had not felt in a long time, as if someone was watching her. Quickly, Margaret whirled around, but found nothing nearby. Taking in a few shaky breaths, she leaned back against the table and braced herself. She had to get over this unmerited fear she continued to have. Nothing was going to happen to her.

Slowly, she turned back around and continued to look at the patterns. After a few seconds, Missus Plumes came out with a bundle of beautiful yellow fabric that Margaret knew was perfect for her kitchen.

"That is it, that is the one. You knew exactly what I would want. I will take eight yards of it."

"Eight, Missus Westcott? Are you sure you need that much?"

Margaret grimaced slightly, then admitted, "I am calculating for mistakes."

She nodded in understanding. "Oh, I see. Don't feel bad, my dear. When I was your age, I wasn't much good with a thread and needle either. It comes with time though. You can be sure of that. All good things come in time."

"I could not agree more," a familiar ominous voice said.

Margaret spun around, that time with no mistake as to why the hairs on the nap of her neck were on end. Struck dumbfounded, Margaret stood rooted, staring at the one man she could never forget.

The duke had found her.

Margaret took no notice of the store owner's puzzled look as she approached them.

"May I help you, Mister—" Missus Plumes waited for a response but got none.

"I will only be in town for a short time. I came to collect something that belongs to me, and then I will be on my way. I saw something through the window that fetched my eye."

"What might that be? I would be more than glad to get it for you."

"As it turns out, once I got in here, I realized that I had left my pocketbook in my carriage. I think I may stop by later to get it."

Witherton stared at Margaret for several seconds before adding, "It will not be long, I promise."

With that, he bowed gracefully and left the store without another word.

"That was an odd one. Those European aristocrats are such an odd breed. They stick out like a sore thumb around these parts."

Margaret did not comment that, if that were true, why had no one mentioned the striking gentleman who had appeared in town.

"I have to be going, Missus Plumes. I will be by later this week to pick up the fabric and the rest of my items. Please excuse me," Margaret said as she rushed out of the store, leaving a surprised Missus Plumes in her wake.

Heading straight for her wagon, Margaret quickly put her hand in her pocket and felt the reassurance of the pistol she had smartly decided to bring along. Witherton was not about to get the best of her again.

Margaret tried to gauge how long she had been in the store and when Henry would be returning to meet her. As she darted worried glances around her, she contemplated what to do. She had to flee. She had to leave immediately. She had escaped him, outrun him before. She would do it again.

"So, you came to the Americas. I should have guessed you would. It fits that wild streak of yours." Nodding to her ring on her finger, he mocked, "It also seems that you wrestled yourself one of those *American* cowboys, have you?"

Margaret felt Witherton's body against the back of her own. Just as Margaret started to move away, he grabbed her roughly around her chest and pulled her back against him.

"Ah, ah, ah, not so fast. You would not want to draw attention to our little meeting, now would you?"

"What do you want? Why can you not just let me be?"

"My, my, are we not self-absorbed these days. You think this is all about you? Well, let me enlighten you. It is not. Once I found you, I wanted to know what I was up against. Was I ever surprised to find out that you married my bastard brother."

Happily, he glared as the shock registered on her face at the mention of her husband. Margaret inhaled sharply and gasped as he cruelly tightened his grip.

"Did you think I did not know about him? You silly girl, you should know by now, I always thoroughly check out my targets. I figured, two birds one stone. He's been a thorn in my flesh for all my life. I can take care of him once-and-for-all and then I can take you back to England with me. I mean, by now, I have become an expert at getting rid of your husbands."

Margaret roughly pulled away, not being able to bare his touch any longer. Turning on him, she whispered fiercely, "Do not dare threaten my family. I swear upon my last breath, if you so much as come near him, I *will* kill you."

"If you were to be worrying about anyone's neck, my dear Margaret, it would be your own. If I cannot have you, no one will."

Pulling out her revolver, Margaret aimed it directly at his heart. "If you come near my family, I will have no qualms about killing you right out in the open. I don't care what happens to me."

"There are worse things that can happen to you than being arrested or hanged," he said, pointedly.

"You make me sick. I cannot believe I ever trusted you or believed any of your lies."

"Yes, well, you did. And it served me well. I was able to end Henry's pathetic life. Once I rid the world of my imbecile of a bastard brother and take you for my own, I will have everything I want."

Margaret, without thinking, slapped Witherton across his smug face with her free hand. "You will never get the chance."

Witherton narrowed his eyes. "I let you hit me once before without repercussions, you were unwise to try it again."

He raised his hand to hit her back, but was halted quickly when Henry came bursting in from the side, catching both of them by surprise. Margaret quickly dropped the gun to her side as Henry stated, "Mother, Tommy's a liar. His frog doesn't jump nearly as high as he said it did."

"Henry, help me into the wagon. We need to be on our way."

"But you said we were going to buy me some candy," he said in a whine, still not realizing the unnatural tension between the two people in front of him.

"*Now*, Henry, and I mean it. Remember what I said

about it always being better to be *over*prepared than under?"

Henry, finally noticing the gun in his mother's hand, quickly jumped up onto the wagon bench and reached behind the flap, pulling out the rifle.

"Sir, I would appreciate it if you would step away from my mother."

The duke's callous smile could only be described as sadistic amusement. Leave it to Witherton to enjoy a boy pulling a gun on a stranger.

"Well done. I see you have far more spirit than your father ever did. With the right guidance, you might become a man not to cross."

Henry's grip faltered as he said, "You knew my birth father?"

"Knew him? I—"

Margaret interrupted him. "Don't listen to anything he says, Henry. He is a liar. We need to leave, now."

Henry helped his mother into the wagon, continuing to keep his eyes on the threatening stranger, and handed her the rifle once she was situated. Then he took the revolver from her and circled in front of the wagon while keeping the gun pointed at the unknown assailant.

As Henry hopped up into the wagon, he said to Witherton, "Mister, I suggest you leave my mother alone, or you will have to answer to my father, Cort Westcott. You won't like a confrontation with him."

"We will see about that, boy."

Henry picked up the reins to the horses and pulled on

them, making the wagon go as fast as possible without risking injury.

"Why was that man bothering you, Mother?"

"I will explain everything later. Right now, we need to get home and get our stuff packed. We have to be on the road by nightfall."

CHAPTER 29

Despite Margaret explaining to Cort what had happened in town, her husband seemed unnaturally calm. When he made no comment to tell her how they were going to handle it, she realized he had no plans to run with her. In that moment, she decided she had to run on her own with the children. When it was safe, if it ever became safe again, they would come back.

Cort walked in to find Margaret packing her trunk with clothes for her, Henry, and Susan.

This whole scenario felt so familiar to Margaret. She could remember both a time in England and in France when she found herself in a panic, hurrying to pack what little she could take with her.

Margaret only gave a momentary glance up, saying

nothing to her husband for she knew there was nothing she could say to make this easy on either of them.

"We are not running."

Margaret glanced up quickly and then replied as she continued packing. "I know. You need to stay and take care of the horses. There is too much at stake here for you. I understand. That is why the children and I will be—" She choked back a sob. "—going away for a while, and when things are safe again, we can come home."

He moved toward her and Margaret shrank back, her confused emotions dictating her body.

Cort did not let it deter him. He grabbed Margaret firmly, showing his resolve. "*We* are not running. Do you hear me? *We*, as in you and me, are going to stand our ground as a family. We are not running from him again."

Margaret looked up at her husband sharply. "You do not understand. If we stay here, he will kill both of us and who knows what will happen to the children."

"I told you, I will defend all of you unto my dying breath."

"And I told you that is what I am afraid of, Cort. I cannot live knowing you died because of me. If it means I have to leave you to keep you alive, then I will."

"You have to have faith, Margaret. God is going to protect us. Witherton is a man of no faith, and he does not have the protection God offers His children. If we stay and fight, we will be victorious through the Lord."

"I want to believe you, to believe God can keep us safe, but I am so scared."

"Then I know what we must do."

"What is that?"

"We must pray."

Margaret was returning from delivering Henry and Susan to her brother for protection. She knew it was only a matter of time before Witherton showed up as he threatened. Cort had stayed behind to prepare for the upcoming confrontation, and in case the duke showed up while Margaret was gone.

As she made her way toward the house, she felt a shiver crawl up her spine as she had earlier in the day at the store in town. Margaret quickly pulled out the pistol she had been carrying since her encounter with Witherton in town.

Clutching it tightly in a fist, Margaret walked over to the corner of the porch. With her free hand, she leaned forward on the railing and looked toward the front of the house.

Seeing nothing out of the ordinary, she let out a sigh. But the relief was short-lived, for from the opposite way she looked, a hand snaked out and grabbed her arm.

Margaret yelped in surprise and quickly brought the pistol up in defense. But she was not ready for what she saw.

"Catherine?" she whispered in disbelief.

With a boastful smirk, Margaret's one time close friend and sister-in-law asked, "Surprised to see me?"

"I would be lying if I said I was not. How... how did you find us?"

Taking the gun from Margaret's hand, Catherine stated, "We will get to that later. But first, where is my nephew?"

"He is out helping his father."

"You mean your new husband."

"I mean exactly what I said, his father."

"Cort Westcott is not Henry's father. I know he is the spitting image of my brother."

"How did you find us? How did you get here?"

Coldly, Catherine stated, "I had help."

"What are you talking about? Who helped you?"

"My husband."

"Wha-what?" Margaret's voice faltered as she tried to put the unimaginable pieces together. "You cannot mean that you married Witherton," she said in disbelief.

"Yes, that is exactly what it means," Witherton said as he stepped out from behind the shadows of the nearby trees.

Margaret tried to step back in shock but was held tight by Catherine's grip.

What sort of nightmare was Margaret having for this inconceivable state of affairs to be occurring? How could her most bitter enemies join together like this?

"What, Margaret? Let me guess, you did not see this coming. Some say that hate is the opposite of love. So if love is strong enough to bind two people together for the rest of their lives, then the same must be true of hate. And we both truly do hate you."

"Catherine, you know how your brother felt about *him*," Margaret cried out. "How could you possibly marry the one man your brother despised?"

Catherine smiled wickedly. "Easily. We have a mutual understanding that this is, at every level, simply a business partnership. I have already produced a legitimate heir for the Witherton title. After we destroy you and take my brother's son, the duke will provide for me handsomely in addition to allowing me to run the Rolantry estate. This will allow us to part company, with only the need to make the occasional appearances to keep up our position."

Who was this cold creature that stood before her? Apparently living with Witherton had had a significantly appalling effect on Catherine. The shy, sweet girl was now gone, and even the hurt, angry young woman who had replaced her had disappeared. All that seemed to be left was this shell of a woman filled with a seething hate. And sadly, Margaret knew that she was the target.

"Catherine, go find the boy. Once you have him, do what you must to secure him. I will deal with his mother."

So he thought of her only as an instrument he used to hurt. He would see that she was far more than that. She was no longer the simple young girl he had faced back in England, nor the fearful young woman who ran scared from France to the Americas.

He would soon see that standing before him was a

mature, strong woman who was not only a fiercely protective mother but also a devoted, loving wife. And whether he knew it or not, love always conquered hate. Her father had taught her that. His lessons would not fail her now. All the important men in her life looked to God, and today, she prayed he would guide her path.

She knew now, in that moment as she faced her deepest fear, that trusting in God completely would be the only way she would survive. She was going to let God win the war for her and use His strength to get through it.

Catherine released Margaret's hand, nodded toward Witherton, and headed off toward the barn.

Slowly, Witherton walked around the side of the porch to the entryway, making his way up the stairs and then over to where Margaret stood, stopping only inches from her.

"Now that we are alone, I think I need to make a few things completely clear. First, what Catherine says is what Catherine needs to believe. She, as you, will be disposed of once both of you have ceased your usefulness. Intriguingly, you have managed to evade me quite cleverly up until now. Getting married was very smart on your part and made you quite a bit more difficult to track down. But I always win in the end, as both you and your husband well know."

"I still cannot believe after all the men in the world, you managed to not only find, but marry, my father's bastard."

"Do not ever call him that again! He is three times the man you could ever dream of being, despite the circumstances into which he was born. He overcame his hardships to become the greatest man I have ever known, while you—who were given everything—stole, killed, and ruined everything you touched. You are nothing compared to my husband."

Witherton laughed sadistically. "Mayhap you are right, but all those things you despised me for doing made me capable of getting to this point, where in one fatal swoop I am going to destroy not only my troublesome bastard broth, but also destroy what is left of Henry Rolantry's contemptible family. I started with Henry, you see, but I will finish with his sister and son."

"You're disgusting. Do you think I will ever let you harm my son?" Margaret asked in a shaky voice, suspecting she already knew the dark, nasty truths he planned to spill out.

"You should know by now, I do whatever I want and no one gets in my way. It was easy enough to do with your first husband. I had never been so happy as when I got the report that the men I hired did their job and ended Rolantry's life. I had hoped you would meet me with greater gratitude for freeing you of the burden of being married to him, but it seemed your sense of loyalty outweighed your own desires. You could not see the gift I gave you, but perhaps now you can."

Was he completely delusional? Did he honestly think she had any feelings for him other than hate?

"You may have killed Henry, but you did not succeed in

killing the love or the memories we shared. You could not erase them no matter how hard you tried."

Witherton growled and retorted, "Yes, but I robbed you of your life together, and that is really all that matters. And I am going to take his son. I have not quite decided what I will do with him. My first instinct, before I met the spirited boy, was to have him meet with an accident on the way back to England, but now, I wonder if I should keep him around to find a way to use that spirit in a way that pleases me."

She could not let him get his hands on her son. The idea of him raising him, turned her stomach. Realizing that he did not know the truth about his own wife, Margaret decided it would be best to reveal it, hoping it would distract him enough that she could get away.

"I am quite surprised that you decided to marry Catherine, knowing the truth of her lineage."

The duke shrugged at Margaret's veiled hint. "I do not see what you find so surprising. She is rather striking, she has the right connections, and even though she was related to Rolantry, her breeding is not completely atrocious."

"I find it more than ironic that the very thing you condemned your brother for is what you married. Let me be blunt. Catherine is not legitimate. Her mother was one of Henry's father's servants. We fooled everyone—including you, apparently—into believing and accepting her as his full, legitimate sister, which means your heir back in England, is no more legitimate than your brother."

"You lie."

"I do not need to lie. The truth is far more potent. Why do you think you never heard of Henry having a sister until after we were married? She had been away at boarding school, to keep her away from Henry's mother who hated the girl. I was the one who came up with the idea to introduce her as his legitimate sister; a decision I have regretted every day since Henry died. The next time you are with her, ask her. And when you do, look her in the eyes. You will see I am telling the truth."

Growling again, Witherton roughly grabbed Margaret by her forearms. Rage beyond anything Margaret had ever seen filled Witherton's eyes as he yanked her into his sinister hold.

"I told you, I do not care about her. Despite what it might appear, I never have been able to get your taste, your scent, your feel out of my mind. And I think, for old time's sake, I will drench myself in you one final time."

Margaret tried to pull away, but they both knew that he was stronger. Instead of being able to defend herself, she was forced once more to feel the onslaught of someone else's will upon her own.

Margaret jerked her head back and forth, trying to avoid his violation, but only managed to get him angry enough for him to slam her backward into the wall.

"Get away from my wife or I swear I will kill you where you stand."

Witherton slunk back slowly and turned to face his hated

brother. Pulling Margaret alongside him, he wrapped his forearm around her neck.

Witherton turned around to find Catherine being held at gunpoint by Cort. However, barely acknowledging his wife's predicament, he stated blandly, "I was expecting you, *brother*. Although I must say, you are a bit earlier than I would have liked."

"Yes, I can see that."

"Your wife is a bewitching creature, but I am guessing that does not come as a surprise to you. She enticed you into marrying her after her long list of admirers in both England and France."

"You should stop talking about my wife, Richard, before I make you stop talking about her."

"Same empty threats as always, it seems. When will you learn that you will never be able to make me do anything."

Trying to distract the duke, Margaret asked, "How did you find me?"

"We found out that you used to have an investigator by the name of Mulchere who worked for you back in France, and when we paid him a visit, we found a file on you by an admirer of yours—Pierre, I think—who had been checking into all sorts of things regarding both of you. Once we obtained the information we needed—rather roughly, I am afraid—we disposed him to make sure he did not have word sent that we were on your trail."

Poor Mulchere. He did not deserve what happened to him.

Witherton asked his wife, "Catherine, where is the boy? He is what I told you to fetch, is he not?"

In a quivering voice, Catherine replied, "It was a deception, my lord. The boy is staying somewhere else."

"I suggest a trade, Witherton—my wife for yours."

Witherton glanced at Margaret and then shook his head. "No, I think I like the way things are currently. You can keep her."

Cort glared at the duke in disgust. "I am talking about your wife, Witherton."

"Yes, well, like all wives, she is merely a possession, and an expendable one at that."

Cort shoved Catherine to the side, saying, "Then let's get this over with. This has been a long time coming."

"I would not be so hasty if I were you. Have you forgotten what an excellent marksman I am? That scar on your shoulder should remind you of that."

Margaret had always wondered where that mark had come from. Cort would periodically rub it from soreness that would sometimes creep up in it, and he said it was from an old war wound. She had always thought he had meant from the military, but now she realized it was from a different type of war altogether—a bitter one that had raged on through most of his life and had driven him from his home.

"Yes, well, I have learned a few things in your absence. I am not the same little boy you used to pick on back on your father's estate. And remember, you do not have your money to hide behind anymore. Out here in the *West*, we are all equal."

Quickly, without any warning, Witherton threw Margaret to the ground, hard enough to knock the air out of her. Then he pulled out a revolver and, with no hesitation, fired his first shot.

Scarcely having time to dive out of the way, Cort ducked behind the bottom part of the porch.

"Come out, my bastard brother. Where are you hiding? I only need one more shot, and then this will all be over," Witherton taunted.

Cort raised his hand to try to block out the sun but shook his head in frustration. Moving quickly, he headed around the house.

Witherton rushed to the side and looked over the railing before whipping around with his back against the wall.

Catherine pulled a gun from her pocket and yelled as she pulled the trigger. "I should have known never to trust you, Witherton." Her aim was off and the bullet completely missed him.

Enraged by her defiance, the duke turned and fired one shot directly into Catherine's chest.

She crumpled to the ground and lay motionless.

Regaining her breath, Margaret pushed herself up off the porch and ran toward Catherine while Witherton was momentarily distracted, looking for Cort.

She placed her hand on the throat of her once dearly loved sister-in-law and realized she still loved her, despite everything. Not feeling a pulse, she realized Henry's sister was no longer breathing. Margaret reached out and gently closed her eyes. Even after all Catherine had done to her, she did not wish to see her dead.

Witherton hollered out over the railing, "I have tied up one loose end. Why don't you face me and let me tie up one more?" Witherton paused for a moment and then said in a goading voice, "What is the matter, Harring? Afraid to face me?"

"Not at all."

Witherton turned around, shocked to find his brother standing behind him with a long candlestick in hand. Before he could react, Cort swung the candlestick down hard on Witherton's hand, forcing him to drop the gun in response.

Growling, Witherton lunged forward and tackled Cort. For several seconds, the two were one tangled bunch on the ground. Cort emerged on top first with his hands around Witherton's throat. From a hidden pocket in his jacket, Witherton pulled out a small, slick dagger and struck up with it. The gash in Cort's chest sent him reeling backward. Before he could recover, Witherton pounced on him and began to choke the life from him.

As Cort struggled to stay conscious, he groped for anything nearby to aid him. But Cort's help came from an unexpected source. Margaret had rushed back to the porch in the middle of the fight. It seemed that God was with them, for when Cort had knocked the gun from his brother's hand, it had slid across the porch, unnoticed by either man.

Picking up the gun, Margaret stood and aimed the sights at Witherton. She thought she could do it, but she realized, she did not want to deal with the guilt of any more killing. Instead, she decided she would rather knock him out with the butt of the revolver and let him face the gallows.

Margaret ran over to where they were fighting and lifted the gun high in the air, but before she could bring it down on his head, he reached out with his left hand and grabbed her ankle, yanking her roughly to the ground. Not only did the impact of the ground knock the air out of her, but it also knocked the gun from her hand.

Cort was almost dead. Margaret could see she had only mere moments before it would be too late to save him. The thought of losing Cort pushed any moral dilemma out of her mind. Hurriedly, she fumbled for the gun but could not find it.

Dear God, please help me! I need you to help me so I can save my husband's life.

Miraculously, her hand touched the cool steel. Margaret reflexively picked it up, aimed it at Witherton's head, and fired. His lifeless body slumped forward onto her husband's chest. Cort began to cough as air rushed back into his lungs.

Stumbling to her knees, Margaret scooted across the porch and over to her husband. She pushed Witherton's body off Cort's torso, giving a fleeting glance to the man she once thought she loved, and who subsequently terrorized eight years of her life.

It was finally over. They were finally free from their past, and they no longer had to be afraid of anyone destroying the life they had built.

Margaret leaned down and gently kissed her husband as he wrapped his arms around her. She was eternally grateful God had given her Cort, a man worth fighting and living for.

EPILOGUE

Margaret looked out the window at her husband, son, and daughter standing next to her brother, best friend, and their two daughters. She felt a peace and love that exceeded anything she had ever felt before. For the first time in her life, Margaret was able to look out a window and find herself looking *at* something, not looking *for* something. God had given her a beautiful family, and they were right outside that window waiting for her to share her life with them.

The past was behind them and only good things lay ahead. There would be trials undoubtedly, but they would persevere through it together as a family and come out conquering.

Margaret was no longer angry about her past. She no longer dwelled on it, but rather thanked God for the good.

He only wanted the best for them; she saw that every time she looked at her family.

Things were different now. *She* was different now. The emptiness inside her was gone. And because of that, she could look to God differently as well.

Margaret smiled and picked up her bonnet. It was a good day for a picnic. She looked out the window and waved to her waiting family.

As she made her way out of her house with a picnic basket in hand, she greeted them. "Good afternoon, everyone."

All of them returned her warm wishes.

"You ready for a wonderful day in the meadow?" Cort asked.

Margaret smiled. "I am indeed."

"How is my newest niece doing today?" Margaret asked Jackie as she looked at the infant daughter in her sister-in-law's arms.

"She's doing good; finally sleeping through the nights, which means we are finally getting some sleep as well."

"And let me assure you, it is a welcome relief," Randall added.

As they made their way down the path, the children ran ahead of them, laughing and playing tag.

"Have I told all of you how much I love you lately?" Margaret asked.

"Every day," Cort answered.

"And twice on Sundays," Randall added in jest.

"Well, I do. I have never been happier in my life. I am so grateful for how my life has turned out."

"Who would have thought we would end up here? Living as Americans in the frontier?" Jackie mused.

"I guess most of these Yanks are not so bad after all," Randall chuckled, as he patted Cort on the back.

"All I know, is that I'm grateful that God saw fit to bring all of you into my life."

Not being able to keep her news to herself, Margaret stopped Cort, and asked, "Can I speak with you a moment alone?"

Nodding, he said over his shoulder to Randall and Jackie, "We will catch up with you in a few minutes." Then turning his attention back to his wife, he asked, "What is it?"

She took her husband's hand and placed it on her belly. "I have something wonderful to share with you." Tears of joy christened the corners of her eyes as she beamed a smile at him. "I am with child again."

A large grin spread across Cort's face as he shouted, "That is the best news ever!"

Leaning forward, he kissed her gently on the lips. "I love you, Margaret."

"I love you, too, Cort," she said, giving him a kiss of her own.

"What is all this commotion about?" Randall asked.

Apparently, Cort's reaction had grabbed everyone else's attention, bringing the rest of the family to gather around them.

"Can I tell them?" Cort inquired.

Margaret nodded.

"We are having another baby," Cort revealed.

"Oh, what wonderful news," Jackie exclaimed.

Randall hugged his sister, then Cort. "We are so happy for the both of you."

Henry came up next and smiled. "I hope I get a brother this time. It would be nice to not have to play tea or dolls all the time."

Everyone began to laugh.

As Margaret placed her hand on her belly, she was grateful for the new life God saw fit to give them. Looking around her family, Margaret felt her life was complete.

Want to find out what happens to Pierre? Grab your copy of The Oregon Pursuit to find out.

SNEAK PEEK OF THE OREGON PURSUIT

1870 West Linn, Oregon
America

Pierre Girald, the Vidame of Demoulin, looked outside the window of the carriage he shared with his friend, Lord William Almonbury, the son of an English viscount. William had talked Pierre into leaving Paris to join him on his trip to visit his holdings in West Linn, a thriving frontier town in the Pacific Northwest part of America. Hoping to entice Pierre into investing in some of the exciting and new ventures the area had to offer, the grueling trip had been presented as an adventure.

Pierre had welcomed the distraction from the concern over the sudden disappearance of the people he loved. Several years prior, he had left Paris to take care of business, as well as to avoid watching the woman, who held his heart, become engaged to another man. When he returned, he found Margaret had vanished along with his cousin, Jackie, and childhood friend, Randall.

He suspected their sudden disappearance had been spurred by the Duke of Witherton, who had been hunting Margaret along with her young son, believing he fathered the child during an illicit night. The duke had been the reason Margaret had fled to Paris and stayed with Pierre while she was hiding.

Pierre had loved Margaret since they were children but their time together in France solidified his feelings for her. He made his intentions known, wanting to court her, but she told him his lack of faith in God made it impossible for her to accept him as a suitor. The rejection wounded him deeply but to watch her quickly become involved with another man made it impossible for him to stay in Paris.

When he returned to find them gone, he immediately hired an investigator to track down their possible location. When some loose leads pointed to America, Pierre agreed to travel with William, with the hope of finding them as he made his way out west. As luck would have it, their common friend, whose family had relocated to Boulder, Colorado, invited them to stay with him before they made their way up north. A chance meeting at a ball led Pierre to finally track his cousin, the woman he had loved for a decade, and his childhood friend down.

It had been devastating to realize that they had moved

on without him. Pierre had half hoped when he had left for England after Margaret's first rejection, his absence would have made her realize how much she loved him. But when Pierre saw the love between Margaret and her new American husband, he knew she would never be his to have.

Several weeks had passed since he last saw Margaret, and yet, he still was unable to shake the melancholy from his heart. Maybe another new adventure was just what Pierre needed to heal his soul.

"There it is, Pierre, the West Linn Inn. They have all the comforts of a proper European hotel. I am telling you, you are going to love it."

Pierre rolled his shoulders and narrowed his eyes as he stared out at the inn. Nothing had met his expectations in the American west. He did not expect this to be any different.

"I find your assurance suspect, as you have made such lofty promises before, only for them not to come to fruition."

"It is not my fault ever since we left Boulder, you have been in a sour mood. You need to stop wallowing in your misery, Pierre."

"Believe me, I have tried."

In retaliation against his sorrow, Pierre began to drink frequently, gamble often, and enjoy the company of as many women as possible. But nothing dulled the ache left behind by Lady Margaret, the former Countess of Renwick. He had resigned himself that he would never feel love again. Pierre had decided once he had finished his business in West

Linn, he would return to Paris, marry a woman with the right title simply for necessity, and hope that children could fill the void he felt in his aching heart.

The wondrous aroma of baking bread filled the air outside the French bakery on Main Street. The clinking of the front door ushered in another patron.

Amelie Leclaire looked up and smiled at her regular customer, the elderly Mrs. Moore, who was approaching the front counter.

"Good morning, Miss Leclaire."

"Good morning, Mrs. Moore. I have your usual two loaves of bread and box of assorted pastries ready."

"Thank you, dear," the kind-eyed woman spoke, as she leaned on the counter while opening her coin purse.

Picking up the bag of items from off the table behind her, Amelie handed the baked goods over to the woman.

"How are you doing, dear?"

It was easy to detect the concerned tone in her voice. Mrs. Moore had been at her parent's funeral two months prior, along with the rest of the townsfolk. Amelie glanced away, not wanting the observant woman to notice the tears forming in the corner of her eyes.

"Thank you for asking. I think I'm managing to keep everything running."

Barely. She was barely keeping the bakery from closing.

She hated what was happening to their family business. The once thriving bakery was quickly declining in sustainability. The bakery had remained closed for nearly two weeks after her parents' death, and even though Amelie had grown up around the business, she had not been prepared to take on all the responsibilities required.

Additionally, over the past month, several mishaps had drained the savings her parents had managed to put away for a rainy day. She was still unsure how the flour got mixed up with the sugar, but the mistake had cost her an entire day's worth of bread and pastries. Added to this was the oven breaking down and supplies going missing from a nighttime burglary; Amelie was worried the bakery would have to close at the end of the month if she didn't figure out some way to make up the lost revenue.

Mrs. Moore handed the money for the baked goods to Amelie, who in turn opened the cash register on the counter next to the display case. Quickly, she realized Mrs. Moore overpaid her by nearly five dollars.

"Mrs. Moore, you gave me the wrong amount. Here let me return this to you."

Amelie reached out and tried to place the money back in the woman's hand but was met with protest.

"It wasn't a mistake, Miss Leclaire. I know the situation you are in. My husband is a member of the board for the bank. I know that your loan is past due. Your parents were pillars in this community. I refuse to let the tragic accident that took their lives also take away all they worked so hard to obtain in order to properly provide for you and your sister."

This time, Amelie couldn't restrain the tears. She took the edge of her baking apron and wiped away the stinging drops, which clouded her eyes.

"You are kind, Mrs. Moore, but I can't take your money. I'll find a way to keep up with the demands of the bakery."

Being the richest woman in town, Mrs. Moore did not need to run any of her own errands. However, for the past several years, she had chosen to come to the bakery in order to talk to Amelie's mother. They had grown rather close over the years discussing town politics, church happenings, local news, and their families. It seemed to be the older woman's social outlet. Mrs. Leclaire was one of the few townspeople who had not been intimidated by Mrs. Moore. Amelie believed she missed her mother, and that was why she continued to come in to the bakery despite the fact her mother had died.

"But what about your schooling? Aren't you supposed to be returning to San Francisco to finish your training to be a midwife?"

"I've decided not to return. My sister needs me here and I refuse to let my aunt take her away from all she knows. She is threatening to take Elise back to Paris if I go back to school. She doesn't think I am capable of taking care of both the bakery and my sister. I have to make this work for Elise's sake."

"Well, your parents would be proud of you for looking

after your sister. But they wanted you to follow your heart, dear, and I don't think they would want you to give up your future like this."

"My parents would understand I'm putting family first. Elise is helping me in the afternoons. This place belongs to her as much as me. I can't just sell it and let my aunt take her across the world where I will never see her again. Besides, we hardly know her. The first time we met our aunt was only two weeks before the funeral."

"I understand all of the history. Your mother told me how your aunt came to town to reconcile with her after their father died."

"My mother only spoke once to me about her family and the reason they left France. It was a source of deep pain for her."

Amelie's parents had met while her father was the head pastry chef at one of the most famous French bakeries in all of Paris. Her mother was the daughter of the owner of the bakery. Additionally, her family owned several other restaurants and bakeries across France. When Amelie's parents fell in love, her mother was forbidden from seeing her father. Her grandfather wanted her mother to marry someone more established in society to increase their station. He refused to give his consent for their marriage.

Secretly, her parents left Paris for America, where they could start a family and open their own bakery, away from the disapproval of her family. They had naïvely taken the harsh passage west on the Oregon Trail, resulting in the death of their baby. They were forced to bury him along the way. The loss of their first and only son took a toll on them. They were never the same after the loss; however, their faith in God had carried them through the pain. It was that same faith they had instilled in Amelie that would help her succeed in filling her parents' shoes.

"Your mother missed her family and wished she could've reconciled with them. She remained steadfast in not contacting them, out of respect for your father. She worried time had not changed your grandfather's opinion of the situation and she didn't want to open old wounds. She was completely taken aback when your aunt arrived and informed her of your grandfather's passing."

"After my parents passed away, my aunt stayed under the pretense that she wanted to help us, but I'm not sure why she insists on remaining here still. She makes it clear she wants to return to her life in Paris; however, she refuses to leave without Elise. She thinks she would be better off there."

Shaking her head adamantly, Mrs. Moore stated, "Hogwash, your home is here. We have known you girls since you were born."

"Agreed. I always planned on making my home here after I finished school. It just seems my future has changed to running the family bakery now," Amelie declared as she gestured around the room.

Mrs. Moore reached out and patted Amelie's hand.

"You always have such a positive perspective on things, my dear."

"I am similar to my mother in that way. She taught me to always look at the bright side of any situation. Difficulties will come, but how we handle those obstacles define us."

"Just remember, my offer still stands. I want to help you and your sister in any way I can."

Nodding, Amelie responded, "I appreciate it, Mrs. Moore. Your care and concern mean a great deal to me."

"I best be getting home to make sure the house staff has everything in hand for dinner tonight. Mr. Moore likes his dinner ready when he gets home from the mill."

Indeed, he did. Everyone knew Mr. Moore liked everything precise. He had his wife run his home just as he ran his business, the Willemette Falls Mill, with an iron fist.

"Certainly, Mrs. Moore. I also included a Mille-feuille for Mr. Moore. I know it's his favorite." Amelie handed over the bag of baked goods to Mrs. Moore.

"You are too kind, dear. He will appreciate the thoughtfulness," Mrs. Moore said, as she headed towards the exit. Pausing at the front door, she added, "I will be in at week's end, for my usual order."

"I'll have everything ready, Mrs.Moore."

"Good day, Miss Leclaire."

Grab your copy of The Oregon Pursuit.

SNEAK PEEK OF LAWFULLY LOVED

Late Spring of 1877
Outskirts of Abilene, Texas

The sun was stretched low across the late-day sky as Deputy Sheriff Jake Bolton pushed his horse through the prairie flats. A herd of Texas longhorns grazed on the thick fields of golden grass along the road as Jake galloped past the livestock.

He heard the screeching sound of a bird above, causing him to raise his hand over his brow to scan the horizon for the creature. Just as he located the white-tailed hawk, it swooped down and snatched up a small creature from the ground. Such was the cycle of life in the rural Texas countryside.

In his head, Jake went over the details of the investigation he was working on which brought him to the outlying small towns that dotted the northeast corner of Taylor County. The third general store in two weeks had been robbed by the infamous Grimes Brothers.

Jake was tasked with following up the newest lead after a local stagecoach company out of Woody, Texas telegraphed the sheriff's office. One of the drivers had seen two men fitting their descriptions on the road between Woody and Rockwood Springs. The brothers were armed and dangerous, and Jake wanted nothing more than to free the county of their threat.

In the distance, clouds were rolling into sight and the smell of rain was in the air. It wasn't surprising since sporadic showers were common during this time of year. He needed to get to Woody before the sun set and he got caught in the downpour.

Exhausted from a long day of work, Rebecca Caldwell used the sleeve of her blue calico dress to wipe the sweat from her brow; grateful to be finishing up the last of the outside chores. She still needed to prepare dinner for the family, but at least she would be inside before the rain started.

After pulling the last shirt from the clothesline, she pushed several blonde curls out of her face which had come loose from her bun while she worked.

Rebecca made her way around the side of the farmhouse which sat on the same property as the family business—the local livery. As she entered the barn-like structure, she looked around and located her father in front of one of the stalls.

"Father, I'm done working outside and wanted to let you know dinner will be ready in about an hour."

Although brilliant with a horse, Mr. Caldwell often got lost in his thoughts while working with them. He needed constant reminding to finish up his work on time as he often forgot to come in for meals.

The middle-aged, thin man with peppered brown hair and blue eyes— the same color as Rebecca's—glanced up from combing down the colt he had been training all day. "Thank you for reminding me. I'll make sure to not forget this time."

With a nod of her head, Rebecca turned around and moved towards the house. She saw her younger sister, Lydia, run past, and a few moments later, her younger brother, Georgie, chase after, calling, "You better find a good hiding place; I'm gonna find you."

Rebecca smiled to herself at the cuteness of her siblings. Lydia was like a miniature version of Rebecca with her curly blonde hair and blue eyes. Being only ten, she still loved dolls and playing games with the local children. Georgie was sandwiched between them at the age of fourteen and was a rascal at heart. He was getting to the age where he was playing less and noticing girls more, but every once in a while, Lydia could still talk him into playing with her.

As she heard Georgie stomping around the yard looking for Lydia, she reminisced on a time—years ago—when she was able to be carefree like that. She had been forced to grow up quickly when her mother's condition worsened. Rebecca had to take over running the family home and caring for her siblings. She justified her lost childhood as preparation for married life; it would make her a better candidate for a wife.

Although not of spinster age at twenty-one, Rebecca knew it was time for her to start considering finding a husband. Life was hard on the Texas prairie and she needed a man to protect her when her father was no longer able to do so. She wanted to marry for love, but the practicality of finding it was not wasted on her. She knew there was a real possibility she might have to settle for a relationship built solitarily on friendship.

As Rebecca climbed the back steps of the house, she heard her brother and sister laugh with merriment. Apparently, Georgie had found Lydia after all. Rebecca made her way into the kitchen where she pulled out several pots and pans to start the evening meal.

The wind howled in Jake's ear as it raced along the back of his neck, sending a shiver up his spine. He had hoped to make it to Woody before the onslaught, but the clouds had other ideas. Jake pulled the rim of his hat down to shield his eyes from the frigid rain pelting his body.

Jake tightened his grip on the reins to his brown and white paint horse, Ginger, as he pulled her to a stop. Up ahead, the rain had washed out part of the road.

With a heavy sigh, he debated what to do. If he backtracked in order to find a route that bypassed that section of the road, it would delay his arrival in Woody by at least a half day. Should he brave it by trying to cross the muddy area?

Deciding it would be better to take his chances, Jake prodded Ginger forward, gently pushing his spurs into the horse's side. Usually an obedient horse, it surprised Jake when she sidestepped and hesitated. Did his horse sense something Jake couldn't see?

With a scan of the area, Jake resolved going ahead was still the best option. Jumping down from his horse, he guided Ginger through the murky water. Coaxing her, he said, "Come on, girl, just a little further. I promise you some primo hay and maybe even a sugar cube or two if you get us safely to Woody by nightfall."

Reluctantly, the horse complied and started to walk along the road behind Jake. The further they traveled, the deeper the mud got until both of them were finding it difficult to move.

Just as Jake worried they would become stuck, a lightning bolt came crashing down right in front of them.

Neighing in fear, Ginger reared up causing Jake to be knocked down. With a hard thud, he pummeled to the ground, knocking the air from his lungs.

The mud sloshed around him, pulling his body deep into its thick grasp. Jake blinked once, twice, three times before he tried to sit up from the murky ground. A sharp pain radiated up his abdomen. Recognizing the feeling, he knew the fall had earned him a set of bruised ribs.

With concerted effort, Jake climbed to his feet. As he turned to find Ginger, his eyes grew round with concern. The horse was whimpering and she wasn't placing weight on her right leg. Jake moved towards her and gently lifted the leg from the muddy water. There was a huge crack on her hoof as well as a deep gash at the first joint. What could have caused such a horrific injury?

He placed his hand into the mud. Below the surface, he felt the edge of something rough and hard. Although he couldn't see it, he was certain it was a large rock, most likely brought down by a mudslide from a nearby hill.

Jake reached out and took Ginger's muzzle into his hands. He leaned his face against hers and whispered, "It's all right, girl. You did the best you could. This is my fault. I shouldn't have pushed you so hard."

With deep regret, Jake contemplated what to do. When a horse broke its leg, there was only one thing to do, but he hoped it wasn't the case.

He tried to swallow the lump of pain in his throat. Ginger was the last connection to his past; a gift from his wife, Marjorie, during their final Christmas together. She had saved up money to purchase the horse for two years, washing laundry at the Abilene Inn.

Lightning cracked across the sky, illuminating the air for just a moment. Not far off in the distance, Jake saw the flickering gas lights of a small town. Maybe Ginger could make it to Rockwood Springs—which was closer than Woody—if he helped her stay off the leg.

As he ran his hand through his hair, he sighed. With a heavy heart, he removed the saddle and attached bag from Ginger to make her load lighter. With determined resolve, he started the walk to Rockwood Springs with Ginger beside him.

Grab your copy of Lawfully Loved.

A NOTE FROM THE AUTHOR

I hope you have enjoyed *The American Conquest* and plan to continue to read more from the Window to the Heart Saga as well as my other books. Your opinion and support matters, so I would greatly appreciate you taking the time to leave a review. Without dedicated readers, a storyteller is lost. Thank you for investing in my stories. If you would like more info, please join my newsletter and get a free novella just for signing up.

Happy Reading!

Jenna Brandt

ALSO BY JENNA BRANDT

Most Books are Free in Kindle Unlimited too!

The Window to the Heart Saga is a recountal of the epic journey of Lady Margaret, a young English noblewoman, who through many trials, obstacles, and tragedies, discovers her own inner strength, the sustaining force of faith in God, and the power of family and friends. In this three-part series, experience new places and cultures as the heroine travels from England to France and completes her adventures in America. The series has compelling themes of love, loss, faith and hope with an exceptionally gratifying conclusion.

Trilogy

The English Proposal (Book 1)

The French Encounter (Book 2)

The American Conquest (Book 3)

Spin-offs

The Oregon Pursuit (Book 1)

The White Weddings (Book 2)

The Viscount's Wife (Book 3)

The Window to the Heart Saga

Trilogy Box Set

The Window to the Heart Saga
Spin-off Books Box Set

The Window to the Heart Saga
Complete Collection Box Set

Mail Order Mix-Up Series-mail order bride books about women venturing out West to make new lives for themselves. What happens when they decide to take a chance on love along the way?

Mail Order Misfit

Mail Order Misstep

Mail Order Miscast

Mail Order Misaim

Mail Order Misplay

Mail Order Mister

Mail Order Mishap

Widows, Brides, and Secret Babies-mail order bride stories with a twist. What happens when a bride arrives pregnant or with a secret child?

Mail Order Miranda

Mail Order Miriam

Secret Baby Dilemma-each mail order bride arrives with a baby or pregnant, and the prospective groom doesn't know until her arrival.

Mail Order Madeline

The Civil War Brides Trilogy-during the bloodiest conflict on American soil, two families struggle in the South to not only survive but to thrive.

Saved by Faith

Freed by Hope

Healed by Grace

Border Brides Series-centered around the Old West border towns and the brides who end up there looking for a new start.

Discreetly Matched

June's Remedy

Becca's Lost Love

Hard to Please

The Lawkeepers is a multi-author series alternating between historical westerns and contemporary westerns featuring law enforcement heroes that span multiple agencies and generations. Join bestselling author Jenna Brandt and many others as they weave captivating, sweet and inspirational stories of romance and suspense between the lawkeepers — and the women who love them. The Lawkeepers is a world like no other; a world where lawkeepers and heroes are honored with unforgettable stories, characters, and love. Jenna's Lawkeeper books:

Historical

Lawfully Loved-Texas Sheriff

Lawfully Wanted-Bounty Hunter

Lawfully Forgiven-Texas Ranger

Lawfully Avenged-US Marshal

Lawfully Covert-Spies

Lawfully Historical Box Set

Contemporary

Lawfully Adored-K-9

Lawfully Wedded-K-9

Lawfully Treasured-SWAT

Lawfully Dashing-Female Cop/Christmas

Lawfully Devoted-Billionaire Bodyguard/K-9

Lawfully Heroic-Military Police

Lawfully Contemporary Box Set

Disaster City Search and Rescue

Step into the world of Disaster City Search and Rescue, where officers, firefighters, military, and medics, train and work alongside each other with the dogs they love, to do the most dangerous job of all — help lost and injured victims find their way home.

The Girlfriend Rescue

The Wedding Rescue

The Billionaire Rescue

<u>The Movie Star Rescue</u>

<u>The Best Friend Rescue</u>

<u>The Ex-Wife Rescue</u>

<u>The Cowgirl Rescue</u>

<u>The Single Mom Rescue</u>

<u>The Pop Singer Rescue</u>

Wild Animal Protection Agency

Come be apart of the adventure, danger, and heartfelt moments with the Wild Animal Protection Agency, where brave men and women work alongside each other all over the world, to do the most risky job of all — rescue injured and endangered wild animals.

Rescue Agent for Dana

Rescue Agent for Sarah

Rescue Agent for Kylie

Billionaires of Manhattan Series

The billionaires that live in Manhattan and the women who love them. If you love epic dates, grand romantic gestures, and men in suits with hearts of gold, then these are books are perfect for you.

<u>Waiting on the Billionaire</u>

<u>Nanny for the Billionaire</u>

<u>Merging with the Billionaire</u>

(Entire series on Audiobook)

Second Chance Islands-What's better than billionaires on islands? How about billionaires finding second chances at life, love, and redemption while on one.

The Billionaire's Repeat

(Free the you join my newsletter)

The Billionaire's Reunion

The Billionaire's Hideaway

The Billionaire's Duty

The Billionaire's Christmas

Billionaire Birthday Club is an exclusive resort—for the billionaire who appears to have everything but secretly wants more. After filling out a confidential survey, a curated celebration is waiting on the island to make their birthday wishes come true!

The Billionaire's Birthday Wish

The Billionaire's Birthday Surprise

The Billionaire's Birthday Gift

For more information about Jenna Brandt, signup for her Newsletter or visit her on any of her social media platforms:

www.JennaBrandt.com

www.facebook.com/JennaBrandtAuthor

Jenna Brandt's Reader Group

www.twitter.com/JennaDBrandt

www.instagram.com/jennabrandtauthor

ACKNOWLEDGMENTS

My writing journey would not be possible without those who supported me. Since I can remember, writing is the only thing I love to do, and my deepest desire is to share my talent with others.

First and foremost, I am eternally grateful to Jesus, my lord and savior, who created me with this "writing bug" DNA.

In addition, many thanks go to:

My husband, Dustin, and three daughters, Katie, Julie, and Nikki, for loving me and supporting me during all my late-night writing marathons and coffee-infused mornings.

My mother, Connie, for being my first and most honest critic, now and always. As a little girl, sleeping under your desk during late-night deadlines for the local paper showed me what being a dedicated writer looked like.

My angels in heaven: my grandmother, who passed away in 2001; my infant son, Dylan, who was taken by SIDS six years ago; and my father, who left us four years ago.

To Ginny Sterling and Jo Grafford, my best writing buddies, my comrades-in-arms, my sounding boards, my voices of reason, my partners in all things author. I love you ladies so much.

To my ARC Angels and Beta Bells for taking the time to read my story and give valuable feedback.

And lastly, but so important, to my dedicated readers, who have shared their love of my books with others, helping to spread the words about my stories. Your devotion means a great deal.

ABOUT THE AUTHOR

Jenna Brandt is an international bestselling and award-winning author who writes historical and contemporary romance. Her historical books span from Victorian to Western eras and all of her books have elements of romance, suspense and faith. She has her own best-selling historical series, Window to the Heart Saga, Mail Order Mix-Up, and Civil War Brides, as well as contemporary series, Billionaires of Manhattan, Second Chance Islands and the Wild Animal Protection Agency. Additionally, she's created two best-selling multi-author series, The Lawkeepers and Disaster City Search and Rescue based off the life of her husband in law enforcement. Both of her books, Waiting on the Billionaire and Lawfully Treasured, were voted into the Top 50 Indie Books of 2018 on Readfreely.com.

She's been an avid reader since she could hold a book and started writing stories almost as early. She's been published in several newspapers as well as edited for multiple papers, and graduated with her Bachelor of Arts degree in English from Bethany College where she was the Editor-in-Chief of the newspaper. Her first blog was published on The Mighty website, Yahoo Parenting and The Grief Toolbox as well as featured on the ABC News, CNN Health, and Good Morning America websites. She's also a member of the American Christian Fiction Writers (ACFW) association.

Writing is her passion, but she also enjoys date nights with her hubby, cooking from scratch, watching movies on Netflix, reading books by her author friends, and engaging in social media with her readers. Her three young daughters keep her busy with Girl Scout activities, going to the mall, and playing at the park where they live in the Central Valley of California. She summers on the Golden Central Coast where she finds endless inspiration for her romance books. She's also active in her local church where she volunteers on their first impressions team.

CPSIA information can be obtained
at www.ICGtesting.com
Printed in the USA
LVHW020305070322
712793LV00015B/195